THE LAWS OF MAGIC ARE SIMPLE.
IF YOU SEEK OUT THE DEVIL, YOUR SOUL
BELONGS TO HIM *FOREVER*.
BUT WHAT IF THE DEVIL HIMSELF DOES
THE SEEKING?

JULIET IS A NORMAL WITCH, TRYING TO
FINISH HER SENIOR YEAR, WHILE
GRIEVING THE LOSS OF HER FRIEND. ALL IS
FINE UNTIL A SINISTER ENTITY KNOCKS
ON HER DOOR AND THREATENS THE LIFE
OF HER AND EVERYONE SHE KNOWS.

THE ENTITY THAT HAUNTS JULIET ASKS
NOTHING MORE OF HER THAN TO
SUMMON A BEING THAT IS FEARED BY ALL.
THE SOULS OF THE IMMORTALS ARE NOW
IN THE HANDS OF JULIET. THE SUMMONER.

0

Curse of the Wicked Born

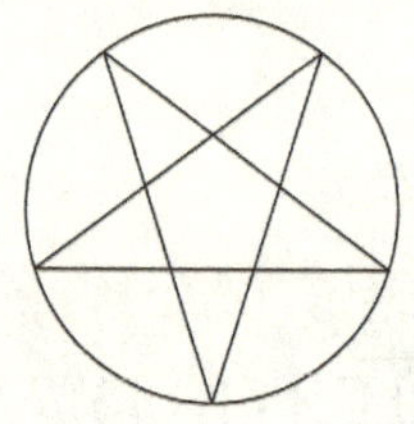

Copyright © 2021 By Sydney J Austin

All rights reserved. No part of this book may be
Reproduced or used in any manner without written
Permission of the copyright owner except for the use of
Quotations in book review

This book is a work of fiction. Names, Characters, places, and incidents are the product of the Author's imagination and are used fictitiously. Any resemblance to actual events, locales, or persons living or dead is coincidental

Cover designed by MiblArt

FOR MY FAMILY, WHO HAS SUPPORTED ME FROM THE
BEGINNING.
TO IRIS WHO HAS CHEERED ME ON THROUGH ALL THE
STRESS. I LOVE YOU.

CHAPTER ONE

It's been a year since I've practiced the craft. Each day without it becomes easier, but the magic still tingles in the tips of my fingers and stirs my stomach. The voice of the unseen and the voice of my ancestors haunt me daily, but I've slowly learned to ignore it. I never thought I could practice again. I never realized how powerful my magic is until the accident. The regret builds inside of me every time it comes to mind. I can't accept the fact that I hurt my best friend.

I'm facing the past and vulnerable to the fear that is slowly taking over my body. I'd like to believe that every day has gotten better, but I lie to myself and choke down the regret. I don't want to be here. The guilt consumes me.

This is not how it's meant to be. This is not how I planned to return to society. I want nothing more than to scream and drain my lungs of oxygen. I want to take my anger out on the smallest things. His body beckons me to dig it up and hug him once more. This anger has filled me from the moment I lost Keelan, and I am the only one to blame.

"Hello, Keelan. I've missed you so much."

The grey stone sits beautifully against the red and golden hues of fall. I've always looked forward to this time of the year, when the leaves turn from green to orange and deep reds. I always had the best memories during this time, but now, as I sit here looking at the headstone, my experiences will be forever changed after today.

The headstone serves as a reminder of the evil I possess. I focus on his headstone, never keeping direct eye contact with his name that is etched into it. Every letter in his name and every number in his birthdate haunts me. They will forever be carved into my mind, almost like a code.

"I don't know where you are, or if you can hear me." I kneel to the ground. "I hope you are at peace. I hope you are okay wherever you roam."

A tear falls from my cheek and lands on a single petal from the bouquet. It doesn't absorb, it gracefully sits there. As I observe the tear, my mind wanders to the deepest parts of myself, and the questions left unanswered. This single tear is full of grief and anger, and many more emotions I've not yet come to discover lie on the most beautiful thing this world offers. You can always revive a flower by deheading it, taking off the old so a new one can grow. But for the mortal souls, we can never get a new life.

I grew up with the idea that every saved soul will rejoice in heaven, and all the non-believers will spend an eternity in hellfire. This belief has also raised questions in the back of my mind. God will only take those who have faith in his power and reject the ones who don't. There are too many pure souls who are damned to hell because they don't believe in the almighty power of God.

Keelan is perfectly imperfect, and the most selfless person I know. He cared for people more than he cared about himself. His enthusiasm lit a gloomy room. Everyone loved him, but he also had his flaws. Many times, he volunteered at the homeless shelter and soup kitchens, all without being coerced into doing it. Those things were done of his own free will, and if that is where free will takes someone, then I want to be where he is. I refuse to imagine his kind soul will spend an eternity in hell and ashes.

"Wherever you are. I hope you are at peace." I pull the grass from the roots." I hope you remember the good times we had, and I pray you are no longer in pain."

I say these things, not knowing or having faith that they will get to him. I wonder if he can hear me, or if some magical being could pass on the message to him. I continue to talk out loud, having an open mind, hoping he can hear me.

The fog encompasses around me, hugging me and relieving me of my grief. The bare trees speak in a language I somehow understand. They send me good thoughts and joyful memories, something I haven't felt in a long time. This leads me to believe Keelan is out there and at peace, whether it be in heaven or another paradise.

A warm pressure settles on my shoulder, and sharp nails dig into my skin. I peer behind me and see deep red nails and wrinkled fingers.

"Juliet, we must go soon." The raspy voice echoes in my ear.

"We have thirty minutes till church starts." I spin around. "Can't you let me have time to grieve?"

She crosses her arms and pouts. "You have been grieving for a while now. I think it's time you return to your life. I think if we went to church early, you could talk to Pastor Kennedy before you return to school tomorrow."

More tears fill my eyes in frustration. Her unsympathetic eyes tear me down. I've lived with this creature since I was born and she has yet to show me any sympathy for my loss. Surely, as a christian woman, she would try to understand. Never once has she shown me she cares. She doesn't know the demons I face everyday just by living with her. It is truly a nightmare living in her shadow.

Anger pulses inside of me, from my belly to my brain. I can feel the word vomit brewing inside me. My knuckles itch to meet her face. I am done being her puppet. I have to break myself from her.

"Can't you let me have this one thing?"

"Oh, Jules." she taps her foot against the soggy grass, "I'm only doing what is best for you. It's not good to dwell in the past."

She caresses my face, and I pull back from her bony fingers. This is nothing more than a show to her. She doesn't have a single nerve in her body to care. She keeps her reputation with the community and the church a priority over me. She doesn't want people to know her as the woman with the psychotic niece. For so long, she stopped conversing with others. She hid herself in her room most of the time. People believed her because she played the victim so well. But she's good at putting on an act.

"No, you are not doing what is best for me. You took away my friends, you cut me off from everyone I ever cared about." I rattle my hands in her face. "Therapy never helped, and neither did those frequent visits from Pastor Kennedy."

Memories from the psychiatric hospital flood through my mind. There are so many days I wished I would have dropped dead. The amount of drugs they pumped through me couldn't have been good for anyone. Every room was the same, white walls with a single window near the ceiling, never big enough for sunlight to show through. It felt more like a jail cell than a hospital.

I remember the day I arrived at the hospital. Edith asked me to go to a church function with her. While in the car, I realized we were heading the opposite direction from the church. She wouldn't tell me where we were until two psychiatric nurses met us at the car. They grabbed hold of both my wrists and guided me to the double doors I would never forget.

She never visited, but she called almost every day, just to see if they cured me. The joke is on her. I'm not cured. It's still amazing how I tricked those doctors into thinking I was okay enough to be discharged.

"When I turn eighteen in a few days, you won't have to worry about me. I'll leave this town."

I say these words without thinking. The words aren't true. I have nowhere to go. I am forever stuck with her. She will never let me move out. I don't even know how I would do it, considering I am still in high school, and it's the beginning of my senior year.

Keelan and I remain surrounded by the dead souls. I don't want to speak, fearing Edith will invade my privacy once more. There are secrets I hold, most of them I'd take to the grave, and some that Keelan holds with him.

"One day, I'll see you again. I promise."

After leaving the cemetery, we go to church. The parking is bustling with churchgoers of all backgrounds. Women wear their long skirts and long-sleeved cardigans, while the men wear button up shirts and dress pants. Little kids wear floral dresses and frilly socks that go with the Mary Janes. I don't want to get out of the car. I know people will stare, and I don't know if I am prepared for that kind of attention.

The minute someone sees me, Edith would roll in and claim she healed me, or even go as far as saying God healed me. If God healed me, then I would not feel this way still. I adjust my hair so it covers my scar.

"Good morning, Edith, and good morning Juliet." Pastor Kennedy smiles. "Great to see you both here on this wonderful Sunday."

Edith and Pastor Kennedy exchange handshakes and hugs. I stand by, keeping my eyes lowered to the ground. If I don't look at them, maybe I'll be less noticeable. But, that has never worked before.

Everyone piles into the sanctuary. The old chairs creak in unison as everyone takes their seats. I'm actually happy Edith doesn't make us sit in the very front like we usually do. I don't want Pastor Kennedy eyeing me the entire time. Sometimes, I believed he knew things I thought he didn't know. While I was away, Edith may have been feeding him lies upon lies.

"Good morning everyone. God bless this rainy Sunday." Pastor Kennedy lays his bible on the stand in front of him. "I want to make a quick comment about one of our members of the church."

Oh, no. Don't say it.

"Our beloved Juliet Arden has returned to us with a full recovery. God has blessed her and her family well, hasn't he?"

"Amen," the audience shouts.

I don't appreciate being put in the spot like that. I would have liked it more if he just went on his rant about how Jesus loves us and if we give ourselves to him, then we'd live in eternal glory.

The entire time during the service, Edith has her bible folded out in her lap, following along to each of the verses Pastor Kennedy has to preach about. She even highlights certain verses that please her. We stand for the choir, and she raises her hands to the air, letting the holy spirit move through her. Her singing is masked by those singing around her. This is the only time I wished I was actually sitting up front, so I couldn't hear her.

I look around, searching for something to distract me from this reality. I look at each face in the sanctuary. I notice a few kids who also go to the same high school as me. It's so hard not to stare, but they stare right back at me and I lose my focus on them.

One girl I did notice was on the sophomore cheerleading team, Carlee Robinson. She is the only person on the cheer team who never bullied me. Her friends encouraged her to chime into the hate they spread. I knew she went to this church. I just hadn't been here in so long I forgot about her. She catches my eye. We exchange soft smiles and return to Pastor Kennedy.

Then, there is Mitchell Young. He shouldn't even be here. If his parents knew how much trouble he causes, he would be in a juvenile prison right now. He was the one to always sneak on alcohol to school, or try to sell drugs behind the school bleachers. I don't know how he could sit between his parents, praying to the Lord. All with a clear conscience.

I observe the audience as all heads are bowed to pray. I squint my eyes, hoping Pastor Kennedy doesn't catch me prying. Each head is bowed, some hold their hands together, and some are rested on the pews in front of them. I see some people mumbling their own prayers, while others listen to Pastor Kennedy.

"I urge each and everyone of you to do God's work. Love each other without judgment and live in Jesus's footsteps," Pastor Kennedy's voice echoes off the high ceiling.

I actually agree with him on his sermon. I usually don't, but maybe this is a special service for me, so I don't feel so bad about people looking at me and judging me. The first thing people always see is my scarred face, and they can never get past that. It's not the staring that bothers me the most, it's the lack of communication that sends me off edge. They stare at me as if I have a disease that's contagious.

After the service, Edith remains in her seat while the others retreat to their vehicles for an after church lunch. I don't want to ask why we haven't left yet, but I knew if I tried to get up, Edith would stop me and preach to me about disrespect in the church. We are always one of the last to leave.

"Are we going to leave? I'm getting hungry."

Edith ignores my questions. She rises eagerly when Pastor Kennedy approaches us.

"What a lovely service." Edith shakes his hand.

Pastor Kennedy pats her hands. He keeps eyeballing me, like he has something to say.

"I hope you enjoyed the sermon too, Juliet," he says.

"Yes, it was very enlightening. The part I found fascinating was when you talked about people walking in Jesus's footsteps. I wish more people would live a generous and kind life."

It wasn't a complete lie; I did pay attention to most of the service. I picked out the parts that I liked. I stopped listening after he told us all non-believers went to hell. I didn't have the heart in me to give him a piece of my mind. I just don't have any more fight in my heart. I have been through enough. Telling him my thoughts won't change a thing.

"Great." Pastor Kennedy sits next to me, but a little too close. "I want to wish you luck tomorrow for your first day back. Just in time for senior year. How wonderful is it to be nearing adulthood?" He laughs.

Edith eyes me from above, to make sure I am listening to him.

"I hope that once you graduate, you will consider going on a missionary trip with the rest of the kids your age."

"Sounds… lovely, Sir."

"I look forward to seeing you next Sunday. And by the way, since I won't see you on your birthday, happy early birthday."

He tries so hard to get me to like him, and maybe I did like him a little more than my aunt. He is so nice when we talk, but I feel his words are fake most of the time. That's how most pastors are, right? They are nice to your face, but have a whole book of what they would really like to say to you.

Chapter Two

I follow behind Edith like a duckling. I keep my eyes down to avoid the hungry predators who lurk in the hallways. They think they are clever, covering their faces, but I hear every word that escapes their mouths. I have mastered the art of heightening my senses by only simple intentions. For days, I have prepared myself for the hateful words and deathly glares that would soon come from the kids I call my classmates.

"They should have kept her in the looney bin."

"How did they let the murderer out?"

"She looks hideous."

Surely, Edith hears what they whisper, but she trudges along the hallway with her head high and proud, and ignores the criticism. I always thought she was ashamed to be my aunt, or ashamed to be seen with such a monster. To her, I'm only a burden. I can't help but wonder, If no one wants me here, then why do I remain?

"Juliet Arden is here to see the counselor," Edith demands.

The woman behind the desk is quiet. She eyes me every few seconds, as if to gawk at my horrid face. I cover my face with my hair so the scar is hidden. The students peer through the windows.

They make it known by their body language that I am not welcome back into their territory. I want to hide myself in a locker.

The office door creaks open, and a man with white hair exits the room. His dull eyes give the impression that he doesn't want to be here either.

"Come on in, Ms. Arden," he sighs.

As we sit here, Edith doesn't hesitate to speak for me. I never have the chance to tell my truth. She wants to make sure I tell the story right, her story. She believes I can't go around telling lies, even though they are the truth. What angers me most of all is that people actually believe her. Even the doctors believe her. You would think a seventeen-year-old girl could speak for herself, but Edith always set the record straight.

"Juliet, we are glad to have you back. We hope your return will go smoothly."

Edith crosses her legs and arms. She doesn't want to be here, and neither do I, but she insists this is for the best. She kept me from school for almost an entire year, but I managed to keep up with the school work despite being locked up.

"You are aware of the incident that happened a year ago, aren't you?" Edith whispers, as to not send me into a panic. It almost repulses her to speak of the past.

"We are aware, and we will help Juliet in any way we can."

"Stop talking about me like I'm not sitting right next to you," I say. "Do you even know what will happen to me once I go through those doors? Those kids are monsters."

They snap their heads at me. Their angry eyes look me up and down. I don't care if I get detention on the first day of school. I cannot allow myself to be treated so poorly.

"Juliet, that is no way to talk to school staff."

"You are talking about me as if I'm not sitting next to you. It's bullshit," I shout.

Edith's eyes almost bulge out of her skull.. Her hands form into a fist as if she would strike me on school grounds. I want her to hit me, just to prove how wicked she really is. *Hit me, please.*

"When I walk out that door, that is the end of me." I shift in my chair and put my hands on the desk. "You think those kids will understand? They believe I killed Keelan."

Edith is fidgeting in her chair. She wants to speak, but holds back her nasty thoughts. The counselor nodded his head as if he cared about my situation. He sits back in his chair, as if inviting me to say more.

"Maybe you aren't ready to go back to school," Edith sighs.

"No, Aunt Edith, you aren't ready. You care more about your church friends than you ever cared about me. I wish my mom was here." I toss my bag over my shoulder. "I can handle myself."

The door opens, and Edith exits behind me. She makes no eye contact with me, but pulls me to the corner of the office. The office people keep their heads down. The kids are still watching me from the hallway window. This is like the perfect drama television show.

"Listen here," she leans in with her rancid breath on my ear. "I know the power you possess. Don't you dare pull any of your little tricks. I will know. You don't need no more blood on your hands."

She departs in a hurry, leaving me breathless with her demanding behavior. Her words scratch in my head like a broken record player. I'd enjoy nothing more than to throw her into the window that separates me from the predators. She knows what I am capable of, but I know deep down she is right. My power is dangerous, and shouldn't be taken lightly. My powers are unpredictable. I cannot lose anyone else, even if it is her. She is all the family I have left.

"Ms. Arden, here is your class schedule," the secretary interrupts.

I look through the mess of a schedule; It is full of math classes and a college English course. I feel I don't need half of these classes, but Edith insisted I take extra classes. I am surprised they aren't holding me back a grade. I have to graduate on time so I can finally leave this hell.

There is a knock on the window in front of me. It startles me and almost makes me drop my papers. I am already on edge today. What else could possibly happen?

The moment I see her face, the weight lifts from my chest. The heaviness of the world disappears. The butterflies swim in my belly. In an instant, joy fills my heart.

"Regina."

I run out the door and embrace her. She breathes on my neck. Her familiar scent fills me with comfort. Her smile, perfect in every way, makes the clouds open and the sunshine trickle through. She is everything I want in this overwhelming moment.

Her smooth hands caress mine. She's the same girl I grew up with and has the same energy she always wears so well. I missed the shine of her blonde hair and the scent of rose petals.

"I am so glad you're back, Jules." She hugs me tight, then let's go softly. "I've been waiting so long to see you again. Your Aunt wouldn't let me visit you."

Her touch lingers on my skin, and my nerves shake with excitement. Nothing is better than this very moment. She swings my hand in hers and our bodies travel along the hallway. I give no attention to the prying eyes surrounding us. The world is non-existent.

We halt in front of the glass case at the end of the hallway. The shelf is lined with green and gold wreaths and flowers, candles and yearbook photos. This is Keelan's memorial. It is my first time seeing the memorial since the accident, and I hope it will be my last. I can't keep my eyes on the picture for more than a few seconds before I start to feel the tears coming through.

The tightening in my stomach returns. I sway back and forth, not knowing how to cope with the scene in front of me. The most perfect picture sits in the display case. It is of Keelan and the three of us, Regina, Brody and I, sitting in the bleachers of Brody's last football game of the season. We had our arms wrapped around each other, smiles plastered on our faces, and the existence of one we have lost.

I remember that day clearly, and I live it inside my head each day. Brody didn't want us to watch the last game. He had no faith in his own team that they would win; he was almost ashamed. I mean, I don't blame him; the team was terrible. Keelan met him in the locker room and talked him through it, almost beating his ass for it. Out on the field, we cheered Brody on till the last second in the game. The team won with winning numbers. I can still hear the crowd cheering.

"Why are we here?" I ask, shaking myself from my trance.

Regina rustles with the flowers, picking them up and straightening them to perfection. Dust flies off the fake petals and into the air. It shows how long the memorial has been here, but no one has bothered to keep it clean. Quite disrespectful, if you ask me.

"I thought you should see this." Her eyes search me for a reaction. "You needed to see this. Isn't this beautiful?"

I glance at the whispering students behind us. I try hard not to acknowledge their existence. I cover the right side of my face, hoping to hide the ugly scars that line it.

"Beat it." Regina motions. The students scatter and bury their faces in their lockers.

"Do people really think I killed Keelan?" I whisper.

Her face turns pale.

"People talk and make up silly rumors, but we know the truth."

I held my hand to my face, feeling the scars surrounding it. I am the Freddy Kruger, adjacent, a vile creature no one dares to converse with. As if I already have low self-esteem, the scars make it no better. I fear my life will continue to go downhill from this point. I can't even enjoy my last year of high school.

"You look beautiful," Regina reassures.

I smile back at her, though it is nothing but a fake expression. I only show her what I want her to see, but I know she can see right through me. I am too easy to read. I haven't mastered the art of masking my emotions.

We stand silently in honor of our friend Keelan. Moments go by and everything is peaceful. That is until I see Regina open her mouth from my peripheral vision. I forgot how often she couldn't stay on one subject at a time.

"Say, your birthday is next week," she smiles.

"No. No way. Whatever it is you are thinking, it's a big fat no."

"Come on, let's have some fun," she pokes at my shoulder. "There's a Halloween dance on your birthday. Isn't that great?"

That word is such an overstatement. I dread my birthday every year. Not because I didn't like ghosts and all things spooky, but I dread it because that's the day my mother died. Aunt Edith would never go into details about her death. She didn't even want to speak of her name. Every year after I was old enough to understand death was never the same. I couldn't fully enjoy my birthday without thoughts of my mother surging through my head.

"I don't know if Edith would let me." I cross my arms.

"Screw your Aunt. She put you through enough hell these past few months. You need this."

The thought of going to a Halloween dance frightened me; all the noise and deranged teenagers. The dancing scares me the most, all because I have two left feet and would certainly make a fool of myself. I also don't want to be around people who only see me as a killer. How could I possibly enjoy myself when they have done nothing but hurt me? I cannot put myself in that type of situation.

"We can dress up and no one would know it is you," she smiles devilishly.

"Fine, I'll go. But I'm not dressing up as a vampire."

***

I enter the classroom with my head down and books in hand. Not many people have yet to show up, but I'm glad because I want to get the very back seat in the room, so no one can bother me. I find it easier to look at the back of people's heads than people looking at mine.

Mrs. Evanston gives me a copy of the history book we will be using for the year. I flip through it to burn some time before class starts. Every few seconds, I can see her eyeing me closely. I know I'm not some masterpiece in an art museum, but more like a freak in a freak show.

The students begin to pile in. As they enter, their faces change, and whisper to each other just like they did in the hallway. I pray that Mrs. Evanston can at least stand up for me and not allow the shit talk. It seems that all kids know what to do nowadays is gossip and bully others for their imperfections.

The kids hesitate to sit in front of me or even beside me. No one wants to be near me. I try not to care, because in all reality, I am not here for petty talk; I am here to learn and graduate. Then, I'll be able to leave this town and hopefully start over.

A few students from the middle decided to start exchanging notes. It's such an elementary thing to do. They pass it back and forth a few times before Mrs. Evanston takes it from them. She brings it to her desk and opens it. Trying to figure out who the note is about, she stares at me and then back at the note. *Come on, don't play dumb. You know who it is about.*

"I will not tolerate bullying in this classroom." Mrs. Evanston crumbles the paper and into the trash can.

The kids laugh quietly, hiding their faces.

"Mr. Davis, would you like to make a formal apology to the student in which this letter is addressed to?"

The kid stops laughing. He shakes his head no. *Wow, way to out himself.*

"That's what I thought. See me after class."

After class, Mrs. Evanston pulls the kid aside. He doesn't look too happy about it either. I smile to myself. I am glad he got caught the way he did. No one likes to be put on the spot during class. Although it may have stopped him from bullying in that classroom, it won't stop him from doing it in the hallways.

Chapter Three

"This dress is too short." I stretch the skirt closer to my knees.

Regina flips out her mirror and checks her makeup, which is already flawless. She straightens the halo on her head and smoothes out her dress. She chose the costumes we would dress in. I had no say in the matter. We are going as a devil and an angel. It is no surprise I'd be the Devil. I didn't think Regina thought through it much, but I went along with it, anyway. She seems too happy for me to disappoint her.

She created the dresses herself. She is an excellent designer, and I hope one day she will put those skills to good use. However, I figured she made my dress to put me out of my comfort zone. The tight red dress comes almost to my knees, extenuating every curve I fought so hard to hide. The stockings make me more confident. It covers more skin. She completes the costume with the famous devil horns. I am everything people made me out to be.

Regina wears an intricate white dress that flows off her body. The dress is made of lace and so much glitter you could almost inhale it. She curled her hair in the finest curls I have ever seen, and her heels are surely from a lingerie store. She stands inches above me. She's only seventeen, and she has the stride of a model.

The students fill the school courtyard, all dressed as creatures of all kinds. There are the typical princesses and naughty police women, and the boys wear togas and vampire capes. No one seems to be original these days, always wearing a different version of someone's idea.

The chaperons check our school IDs at the door. They move so quickly I don't think they are really looking at anyone's IDs, so anyone could easily slip in.

Fake spider webs, and strobe lights that hang from the ceiling. It was a great setup, but boring after years of having my birthday on Halloween. It was always the same setup. Never enough to scare me. I was hoping for a little thrill. But, it is a school dance, there will never be anything fancy.

"Happy birthday, Juliet," Regina shouts.

I reach out to cover her mouth, but I am too late. People stare and roll their eyes.

"What happened to not drawing attention to me?" I snap.

She giggles and skips to the gymnasium where the party is at.

Music blasts and lights flash into purple and orange. Strangely enough, my favorite colors. Animated ghosts hung from the ceiling, and plastic skeletons line the gym like an army of the undead. I can't help but think it is all for me, but sadly it isn't, and people couldn't care less if it's my birthday.

Over at the snack table, a group of boys dressed as roman warriors huddle around the punch bowls.

"Just a little."

"Hell no, put the whole thing in."

A boy tries to conceal a metal flask, likely filled with cheap vodka from their father's alcohol cabinet. No chaperone is in eyesight. All I can think about is the boy getting away with spiking the punch. I feel so sorry for the unfortunate students who will fall victim to their mischievous ways.

"So disgusting," I shout.

Regina wears a look of evil in her eyes. As she looks at the punch bowl, she smiles. I already grasp what she's thinking. I missed her so much I almost forgot how sneaky she could be sometimes.

"No. No way," she says, pulling me to the table. "What if we get caught?"

If there's one thing that Edith has taught me right, it's to never drink before the age of twenty- one.I have always respected that rule, out of the many she has made. But today is my eighteenth birthday, and breaking the rules sounds so enticing.

"We won't, if you keep your mouth shut. Come on, let's have fun."

She grabs two cups and pours a hefty amount of punch into them, almost over filling it. I lift the cup to my mouth and instantly smell the alcohol. Vodka. It's stench almost makes my stomach turn.

"Cheers." She raises her cup, spilling the punch onto the floor.

"Cheers."

Regina can't stop moving. She isn't dancing, but she is swaying in soft motions, her hips moving and her arms dancing above her head. She doesn't care how ridiculous she looks, and her smile never leaves her face. At least I can have fun watching her make a fool of herself.

"Want to go dance?" she shouts.

My eyes scan over the dance floor. Most of the students are dancing or huddling in their categorized groups. It is heavily crowded, with almost no space for more people. The school has too many students. I'm not sure if I want to be that close to people this soon, people that don't accept me already.

"No, I am just going to watch for a while." I look around for an empty table. " I'll be over there." I point to the table near the exit.

"Boo. Okay."

I watch as she dances across the room, cup in hand, like she is already drunk. I laugh uncontrollably. Regina stumbles into a group of girls, spilling the red punch on another girl's dress, but Regina laughs it off. The girls run off in a hurry, crying with their makeup running down their faces.

One girl I recognize is Meredith Chung. I remember her being on the cheer team during our sophomore year; she had the biggest crush on Keelan. After every game, she would always congratulate him on the win, if our team ever won. Keelan was so nice. He'd never turn her down for a hug. After a while though, she gave up trying to get with him. Keelan was just too nice for his own good. He didn't want to hurt her, but she was crushed.

The DJ plays some great tunes. I am half tempted to request a song, but I don't want to draw attention to myself. Besides, I don't think most of the students here would be okay listening to The Used or Deftones. Not everyone was so accepting of the loud and rhythmic music people called "screamo". It was almost embarrassing to call it that.

A group of boys emerge out of the group of sweaty dancers. They laugh and shout, making each other riled up. One boy dresses as a cowboy, and the others are a mess of a bunch.

"Juliet, is that you?" A voice calls. I can't see well, they are all silhouettes to me. The deep voice, however, sounds all too familiar.

"Juliet Arden. It's been some time."

He comes into the light, and a tall boy dressed as Freddy Krueger approaches me. My heart drops as I notice who he is. I am not ready for this conversation. The exit was right there. I could make a run for it.

"Brody," I hesitate. "I didn't know you would be here."

He takes a seat next to me. I smell the vodka and weed on his breath. My nostrils flare, and I almost cough, but I hold it in to not show my discomfort. I fake a smile. I search for Regina in the crowd, but she isn't in eyesight.

"Of course, I still go here. Senior year, you know. I made the quarterback this year," he laughs.

I smile to make myself look good. I am becoming uncomfortable in his presence. His friends try to huddle around us, but he pushes them away. My heart is racing and the anxiety builds. I can still make a run for it if I wanted to.

"I didn't think you would come, considering it's your birthday. Thought you might be out ghost hunting." He shouts over the music.

As fast as he can think, he blurts out words. I have to keep my cool to avoid doing anything I might regret later. He really thought I'd be out ghost hunting after Keelan passed. What an inconsiderate asshole.

"Yeah, Regina begged me to come. She wouldn't let me say no."

Brody's friends go back into the group of dancers. They are unaware that Brody is absent.

"So, what brings you back to good ole Cambridge, Massachusetts?" He takes a big gulp from his cup. The liquid lingers on his lips.

I can see he isn't entirely interested in why I came back to Cambridge. His eyes wander all over the room, never keeping direct eye contact with me. He fidgets with his hands as if he is eager to see someone. There is no hope for him. He was never like this when Keelan was here. In fact, he was the complete opposite. He was a better person with Keelan around. Brody was a good boy, always got good grades, and never attended parties with alcohol.

He has completely changed himself, all to impress his idiotic friends.

"My Aunt thought I needed to resume my life after," I gulp. "the accident."

He nods.

"Listen, I know things are rough, but I want to clear the air right now," He breathes. " I want to apologize for abandoning you and Regina when Keelan died."

He suddenly trembles in his voice. His emotions are troubling him, and he regrets what he has done. I laid my hand upon his to let him know I understand his emotions. As much as I wanted to forgive him, a voice tells me the apology is not genuine. He has done something so wrong, and something I never thought he would do. He abandoned me at a time when friends needed each other most. That is not friendship. Friends don't leave each other after life changing events.Atleast, true friends don't.

He glares at me with sadness in his eyes. There is nothing more important to me than for the both of us to feel the solace we both deserve. We both know it is time to get past the heartbreak in our life. I wasn't able to be there to help him grieve. My Aunt separated me from Regina and him. Maybe if my aunt wouldn't have put me in a psychiatric hospital, we all three would have been able to grieve properly and I wouldn't be feeling the way I do now.

Swiftly, he leans forward and lays his warm, chapped lips on mine. His sweaty palms caressed my cheek.

"Brody, what are you doing?" I push him back, making him spill his drink.

"You bitch." He wipes the drink from his shirt.

I stand up with pride. He is much taller than me, but that doesn't stop me from being superior to him at the moment. The monster in me emerges, and my devil costume only makes me look the part.

I touch my lips. The pressure from his touch still lingers, and the residual liquor that clings to his lips. I am stunned for a brief moment, trying to think of any reason he thought kissing me may have been a good idea. Rationalizing is too much to handle right now. All I feel is vexation towards Brody. *He kissed me, then got mad at me at my reaction. This doesn't make sense.*

"I just missed you."

"I was in the hospital, I was mentally ill." I cross my arms and try to get a glimpse of Regina. "You never bothered to even visit me once. Sorry I couldn't get over the death of our friend as easily as you did. You asshole."

I don't want to waste anymore of my breath on him. I thought he changed. I want to believe he bettered himself, but I cannot ignore the fact that he is like the boys I have tried so hard to avoid. I have to get out of here, before anymore attention is drawn to me. This moment probably tainted the rest of my highschool year. This is the cherry on top of my birthday cake

I dart through the gymnasium doors.

"Juliet, I am sorry," he shouts from behind.

I find an unoccupied restroom down an abandoned hallway. The music is still loud, but muffled. The lights above the sinks rattle to the vibrations. I wince at the brightness of the overhead lights and I can hear the faint hum of the electricity. I pull my hair back and fan myself to cool off. I struggle to get a powerful stream of water out of the waterspout before I splash it on my face.

I have to take a moment to piece together the events of the evening. *Brody is drunk,* I keep telling myself. He wouldn't do this in any other circumstance, it just isn't him. But then again, the horrible things he said to me after Keelan's death can never be forgiven. I gave him too much hope. I don't regret hating him.

I let the water soak into my skin. I smear the makeup Regina applied earlier, but at this point, I don't care. I don't want any trace of his DNA on my body. I vigorously scrub my lips with water and soap, making my lips red and swollen, and burn all the way around my mouth. It still looks like I have lipstick on.

Click. I jump and grab onto the paper towel sticking out of the dispenser, all while my eyes are still shut. I listen patiently for another sound. My hands shake as I grip the towel too tightly. I wipe the water off of my eyes, making my eyes blurry.

"Regina, is that you?" I tremble.

Click. I spin around and face the door. I wait. My hands shake.

"Brody, If that's you, stop playing your sick games."

I breathe to keep myself calm and toss the towel in the bin. I attempt to open the door, but the handle is stiff. I jiggle it. The lock won't budge. I panic, and anxiety rolls over me like a tsunami. My fight-or-flight senses take over. I continuously rattle the door handle. It is completely frozen. My hand becomes too sweaty to grip onto the door knob anymore.

"Hello, someone help me," I bang on the door, hoping someone will hear my cries.

I listen for anyone walking by, but all I hear is music. No one hears me. No one knows I am trapped. Someone must have locked the door from the outside when I entered. Someone must have been watching me. I don't remember anyone following me, and if it was Brody, I would have heard his heavy footsteps.

"Help m—"

"Juliet, stop."

I freeze. I become distracted by the muffled pumping of my blood. I fear my ears lie to me. There can't possibly be anyone in here; I checked all the stalls when I entered. There is no one here. I look up at the wall above the sinks. My stomach churns at the sight of a cracked window, just big enough for someone slim to fit through it.

"Please turn around."

I feel the vomit sit in my throat.My cheeks burn and my head spins so much I might fall over.

"You aren't real," I whisper.

Without thinking, my body turns itself to face the mirror. The bile rises more into the top of my throat and it burns. I can't believe it. I don't want to believe it to be real. It's a distorted version of the friend I had lost. It is not logically or physically possible that he could be here and in the flesh. He is dead. I saw his dead body.

"Keelan."

There is no sign of emotion on his face. He is within touching distance, but I don't reach out. I am terrified of him being a part of my imagination. Is he really standing in front of me? He could be a ghost of my memory, or an actual ghost coming back to haunt me for what I did.

"Yes, I am here and in the flesh, Juliet," He takes a step forward, sending me tripping back.

He catches me by my lower back. He is real. Maybe I am imagining all of it; maybe it's the vodka warping my mind. He can't be here. I watched him die. I watched his body burn. I left him to die. His death was all my fault.

"What are yo—"

"You need to listen to me. Do not go home tonight. Do you hear me?"

I can't conjure up the nerves to speak. I am too distracted by his very existence. I see him before me. He appears perfectly fine, as if the fire didn't burn him to death. His skin is more pristine than it has ever been, a radiant complexion that once burned has been restored. There is something strange about his skin. There is something about him that I have never noticed. There is more color to his lips. More than when he was alive. They have a reddish tint to them.

He stands tense in his masculine ways. His hair the same, his eyes the same. Nothing has changed about him. He comes across impatient and fidgets with his hands and touches something in his pocket. He keeps eyeing the door as if someone will enter and he can't be seen.

"I need to know you can hear me," he demands.

He shakes me out of my trance. Without saying anything, I nod softly.

"I can't be here long. Please hear me and do not go home." He walks past me towards the window. "Your life is in danger."

Please don't leave.

"I have to leave." He lowers his head and holds out a small vial of liquid. "Here, take this."

"What is this?" I observe its contents. The liquid splashes around.

"Something that may save your life."

Chapter Four

Quicker than he arrives, he is gone in an instant. The window is now closed and shut tight. I must have been paranoid. I am breaking down, and my heart flutters uncontrollably. I have to pound on my chest to make it return to its normal beat. When I look in the mirror, my eyes are heavily dilated. My mind is in a haze, and everything feels like a dream.

The door is suddenly unlocked. I don't bother searching for the person who unlocked it. I storm out, running down the hallway, the click of my shoes echoing off the walls. I have to find Regina. I can't tell her what just happened. She will think I've gone mad. I have to tell her something. Surely she must have been looking for me.

In the gymnasium, people are still dancing to the beat of some pop song. Laughter comes from all sides of the room. I hear a familiar voice by the table I was sitting at earlier. Brody and his friends laugh together. I hear my name called from a boy's mouth. No doubt they are talking ill of me.

"Brody!" He turns around with a drink in his hand and a wicked smile on his face. The squad of boys follow behind him like little ducklings.

"What did you do?" I push him into his friends. People begin to stare.

"What are you talking about?" He glances at his phone before returning to me. "Have you been crying?"

I can't tell him that I saw Keelan. He and the whole school will think I've gone mad. I can't make it worse for myself than it already is. I have to make up a lie.

"Someone told me I am in danger and I shouldn't go home." I gasp for air. " This has your name written all over it."

Silence falls on the faces around them. It is deafening. I've now done the one thing I tried to avoid. And that's to bring attention to myself. The music continues to play, but eyes are on Brody and I.

"What kind of game are you playing? Using Keelan to get back at me?"

Regina emerges from a crowd of dancers. She attempts to stop me from going too far. Her eyes are glazed over, but I see in her face she understands what is going on, and she has to be in on it too.

"Juliet, Keelan is dead. Don't you remember? You killed him," Brody says.

The room spins and I can't hold my balance much longer. I don't want to, but I have to let go. With so much anger stored up in me, I can't control the urge that tickles my fingertips.

"So you are the one who started the rumor that I killed Keelan. You are some low life human. How could you have called us your friend? I hope you rot in hell."

The room is shaking and rattling underneath our feet. The lights above us sway side to side and clink together. The lights flicker in unison with the strobe lights. The light bulbs burst with anger and the glass shatters to the floor. People shield their faces and cry in fear. I know I've started this, and I'm trying so hard to keep my cool. I'm so angry I can't control this.

The cup in Brody's hand shakes violently. The punch splashed out of his cup. He looks at me with worried eyes. He knows what is coming for him. His eyes filled with fear and guilt.

Do I do this? Do I expose myself to this hateful crowd? They treat me like a criminal and belittle me every moment they have. They have no respect. They don't know the true story, and they don't even bother to hear it from me.

"Don't do this," he begs.

"Come on. Calm down," Regina says calmly. "What was all of that about?'

The cold of the night wakes me. The screaming from inside rings in my ears. Strangely, I find enjoyment in others' fears. Maybe they should be scared of me, so I wouldn't have to suffer. I can be the villain in my own story. I don't know how much more of this I can handle.

"It doesn't matter. I have to go," I whisper.

She holds my shoulders, trying to calm me. She brings me back to reality with her choppy movements.

"I'm so sorry." She keeps trying to get in my face. The smell of alcohol radiates off her breath. She's intoxicated.

"Regina. I am going home. Alone." I break free of her grip.

"I'll go with you."

"No, this was a bad idea. I want to be by myself," I reply.

I feel her eyes penetrate me, but I don't look back. I don't want to see her. Nobody should be around me. I'm too destructive. This only proves Edith right about me. I'm not ready to come back. My powers and my emotions clash too much to work together. I thought I could handle this all by myself. The coping skills the psychiatric hospital gave me didn't work. Or maybe they are all bullshit.

I walk down the street, and Regina disappears before I make it off the school grounds. As I walk further up the street, the music fades into nothing. No cars drive by and the children retreat to their homes. I am alone, but something surrounds me; an energy that is insidious all on its own.

I could see my house from where I am. The porch light barely gives off enough light to ignite the walkway. Under the dim light, my home seemed alien to me, like it isn't mine. There is something about the aura that made me not want to enter, but despite Keelan's alarming words, I have to step foot inside. I have nowhere else to go.

I fumble in my purse for the keys. The porch light is so dim, finding my keys is damn near impossible. As I turn the key through the lock, I expect Aunt Edith to be standing in the foyer. I am ready for her to bombard me with questions and punish me for something I didn't do.

All the lights are off, even the light over the sink is off, and it's usually on. The ticking from the clock doesn't make the noise that keeps me up some nights. It's frozen in time. Everything is still and quiet. The ringing burns through my brain.

My head throbs with a stabbing pain. My vision had blurry spots and every time I rub them, it gets worse. My entire body aches. Then I realize the tingling in my fingers and the voices in my head have ceased. I let out everything I tried to keep inside. The power built up inside of me for so long, I now feel a great release. One thing is for sure, I hurt people tonight, and it only proves I'm a danger to myself and others.

I can't help but think of the repercussions I'll face if Aunt Edith ever finds out what I have done. Magic is forbidden to her, and not only that but also a sin. I know I will eventually have to face her. She can't see me dressed as the Devil, especially in her own home. She would disown me and start praying over me, no doubt. After tonight's actions, Edith will be the end of me.

Edith's bedroom door is shut. Her door is decorated with handmade crosses of all designs. I tiptoed across the hallway to avoid waking her. I'm really not in the mood for another sermon.

I think back to Keelan's warning; to not go home. I'm home and I am fine. There is no danger and no one to harm me, except maybe Edith's wrath. I'm starting to doubt I really saw him. I could have been hallucinating, which must be a side effect of my anxiety medication. I can't tell Edith what happened either. I would risk being sent back to the psychiatric hospital.

I uncover the altar in my closet and admire the set up. I straighten the chalice and the stones that surround it. I carefully light the candles on each side of the table. The fire brightens my view of the table. Samhain is almost over and I have almost forgotten to pay my respects to the dead. This year will be the first that I acknowledge two dead loved ones.

I reach for two pictures, one of my mother, and one of Keelan. I stare into the eyes of Keelan. I miss the vibrance of his eyes, and how you could see his emotions through them. His eyes are unforgettable, the green hues are like none other. I think back to when I saw him tonight. His eyes looked more black than green, nothing like I have seen before. Maybe it was the poor lighting in the bathroom, or it wasn't actually Keelan. I could be living in a nightmare right now.

Keelan's photo is my favorite, though. It was taken during sophomore year. We were at a coffee shop together after school, and I caught him off guard by taking a picture of him as he was sipping his drink.. His eyes peek through his dark hair perfectly, but just enough I can see his eyes in clear sight. He wore a letterman jacket of green and black, dirty around the sleeves because his art pen smudged so much.

This is the only picture I have of my mother. Edith claims to have lost all the others she had. My mother and I are very similar. We both have long raven hair and eyes bluer than the sea. I really had nothing to compare my looks to though, considering I don't know what my father looks like.

"As the veil closes soon, I pray you are at peace. Please guide me through life, living it to the best I can."

I let the flames burn until they became nothing, and the wax is a hot pool. I feel only a slight relief during the honoring, but I am still unsettled by the events at the dance. I want to forget it all, but flashes of his face penetrate my mind.

My bed has never felt so good. The coldness of the sheets feel like I'm swimming in the arctic sea. I'm too relaxed to change into another outfit. My eyes become heavy, and it's getting harder to keep them open. My body and mind need to rest.. I sink into the bed and let my mind drift into the abyss.

***

I wake up to the sound of crashing glass. I jolt, and my head spins left and right. It takes a few moments to regain my vision and consciousness. The sound from moments earlier rings in my ears, making it almost unbelievable. I keep myself calm; I am most likely experiencing effects from the spiked punch, or a dream I can't remember.

Another loud noise comes from downstairs. I listen for Aunt Edith's door to open, but I don't hear the creaking. Waiting becomes unbearable. I hear shuffling in the kitchen. Pots and pans clank against each other. Heavy footsteps thump against the wood floor, vibrating the entire house. The steps are too consistent to be an earthquake.

I run out of my room and open Edith's door. The lights blind me. Her bed is perfectly made, and no wrinkles cross the bed. The Bible on her bedside table sits unmoved, and her church clothes lay neatly on her chair. She is not here. I start at the top of the stairs, staring into complete darkness below.

"Edith, is that you?" I call.

The crickets chirp throughout the house. She is nowhere to be found. I doubt she even came home from her Bible study group. I continue to search the top level of the house before I hear another noise from below. Shuffling and creaking echoes through the house. It's not Edith.

I shuffle to my phone on the bed. Dead. I grab the nearest thing I can use as a weapon; a wide limb I found when I was ten. I never knew why I kept it for so long until this moment. I hold my guard up and continue down the stairs, glaring into the sea of darkness.

I find the light switch and prepare myself for what I would find. Everything remains the same as when I returned home. There is no broken glass, no door open. It's as if I was losing my mind all over again.

The creaking starts at the top of the stairs. I had left the light off, so I couldn't see anything.

"Who's there?" I call.

I stare up the stairs, eyeing the light switch ahead of me. I reach the top of the stairs and the shuffling returns suddenly. Shadows creep along the wall across from me. The creaking and footsteps become louder and boom like missiles landing.

I step backwards, almost falling down the stairs. I barely catch myself on the handrail. My heart skips a beat. Looking up, a mass of hooded figures slowly trudges through the hall. They are abnormally tall, and their hoods hide their faces. I see no details of the intruders, but the thought of the unknown raises terror inside me.

Thoughts of Keelan's warning run through my head. How could he have known danger would be here? I am beginning to doubt everything in life. I don't know what to do.

"Who are you, people? What do you want?" I shout.

I am paralyzed. I eye the front door, hoping I can make a quick escape. With the adrenaline running through me, I dart to the door. The handle is steaming hot and welded to the door. Nothing I do makes the door budge. I glance behind me and the hooded figures are now in the living room. A low humming fills the room with a vibration.

The noise is deafening in my ears. I press my hands against my ears tightly, trying to get any relief from the banshee-like sound. I pound my hands against the door, hoping someone could hear me. The hooded figures consume the house on all sides. I am trapped in one corner. I can't escape anywhere I search.

My mind is running in circles. I fear my life will end at any moment. I turn to face the figures who stand feet away from me now. My hands rest on the door behind me. I press my back against the door.

The house becomes abnormally hot; hotter than what humans could survive. The air is becoming unbreathable and suffocating me to no end. Sweat runs down my face and into my eyes. I knew sweating so quickly won't be so good for me, I'd easily become dehydrated.

The humming ceases, and the hooded figures halt in front of me. They stand like statues, as if waiting for something to happen. I struggle to move my toes. My muscles are not moving. Every muscle in my body is rigid. There is no escaping the bond between the door and I. It's as if my body has one with the door.

A robed figure steps forward, inches away from my face. The creature's rancid breath spreads inside my body. No sound can escape my mouth, not even the slightest hum. I can't call for help. The figure grumbles behind its sharp teeth. He raises his decomposed hand near my face, his claws graze over my skin. His claws travel on my face, down my arm, and then to my hand. He snatches my hand in his, cutting off circulation and almost shattering my bones.

I want to cry. I can feel the tears burning behind my eyes. No one can hear my cries. Whatever hold they have over me will surely cause my death.

Please, stop.

The roughness of his hands disappears. A burning sensation runs through my arm and fingers. My stomach twists and I can no longer bear the pain. I can't conjure a scream to let anyone know I'm in distress. Soon, the smell of burning flesh invades my senses. I look down at my arm. My flesh is burning.

I feel a breakthrough; the bond is separating. It's like an unseen force is fighting its way through death. He lets go of me, and I fall to the floor, clutching my hand to my stomach. Catching my breath, I gaze at my bloodied hand. A familiar, yet sinister symbol is embedded in the inside of my arm. A pentagram in its purest form. The mark of the beast. They have marked me.

A lump in my chest formed, a hard and uncomfortable lump. I searched through my dress pocket for the vile Keelan gave me. How could this clear liquid help me? I didn't even know what it was, but he had to have done it for a good reason.

I quickly opened it and threw the cork to the floor. The figures are inches from me now. They chanted in some language I couldn't decipher.

Holy water.

I swing the vile across my body and the liquid splashes onto the creatures. The humming ceases, and the chanting becomes cries of horror, like something straight from hell. As the liquid seeps through their robes, the smell of rotting flesh consumes the house. Their skin burns under their robes. They convulse below my feet. I cover my ears and watch them suffer.

Their bodies melt into the floorboards, becoming nothing but empty pieces of cloth and ash. The cries fade into white noise. The only evidence of their existence lay within the threads of their robes. I'm scared to move. I can't be sure if they are really dead or if I only injured them for a moment.

The expansion of my lungs hurts my chest. My hand throbs with pain, and it travels up to my entire arm. My arm is gruesome. Blood and puss ooze from the burn. I don't know how I'm going to hide this from Edith. I can't just tell her demons came inside the house and gave me a gnarly burn. She would never believe it.

I head to the kitchen and rinse my arm under cool water. It's relieving and painful at the same time. Blood fills the sink, and I try to scrub it away with bleach. I find gauze and medical wrap in the junk drawer. I slather antibiotic ointment across my arm and gently wrap it.

Knock Knock Knock

The front door rattles the house. I check the porch light; it is off. I flip the switch up and down, but the light must have blown out. There is no way of telling who is knocking or if anyone is really there.

The doorknob turns slowly. I search around for anything I could use as a weapon. A lamp seems like a pretty good idea.

"Whoever you are, leave now or I am calling the police," I threaten.

The doorknob is still turning; I press my body against the door, attempting to fend off anyone trying to intrude. I look at the robes on the floor. No one can see this, especially Edith. I have to hide them, and hide them fast.

The jiggling stops, and I hear voices outside the door. I can't understand what is being said. The talking is muffled. It sounds like two or more people are at my door.

"Leave now," I pant .

The door bursts open off the hinges, causing me to fly onto my back. My head hits the hardwood floor. Debris flies through the air. The door lands inches away from my face. I scurry to sit up and watch two people enter the house hastily.

"Please don't hurt me." I raise my arm in desperation.

One person comes towards me with open arms and the other flips the switch on the lamp behind me. I am blinded momentarily.

"Juliet, calm down." Hands travel on my shoulder, but I continue to flail my arms, not seeing what is right in front of me. My head hurts too much to focus.

"I'm not going to hurt you, please stop."

The voice is soothing and familiar. My eyes adjust to the light above me. A silhouette of a girl stands over me with a stern expression on her face.

"Shut her up before a neighbor arrives," the girl hisses.

I sit up and rub my eyes and slowly crawl back on my elbows.

"Keelan. How ar—"

"I warned you not to come back home. Are you okay? Did they hurt you?" He panics, looking me up and down for any evidence of injury. I raise my burnt arm. He cradles it in his and studies it. His eyes glaze over in a panic.

"Shit."

I stare at him like I've seen a ghost, and I probably am. I'm losing my mind and drifting further from reality. Every move he makes made this reality seem like a dream. Nothing seems real anymore.

"How are you here? Who are you?" I glance over at the blonde bombshell on my right.

The shadows shift across her face. And the details are unclear. She stands over me with her arms crossed. Her unpleasant odor of department store perfume distracts me from what is happening in the present. The smell is almost tantalizing.

The feeling is like lucid dreaming. Everything is hazy and dream-like. I try to pinch myself, but all I feel is pain all down my body. If I'm not dreaming, then this is an actual nightmare.

"We have to get you out of here," he pats my back. "I told you not to go home."

His expressionless eyes meet mine. My mind races; I am in a trance. It is too hard to shake it off. I lock my eyes on him and it is almost too good to be true, but here he is. He stands over me in a panic. The sweat drips off his forehead and onto my cheek. *This is real.*

"You knew this was going to happen," I scream. 'How did you know those creatures would be here?"

"I didn't think you would be dumb enough to go home," He says calmly.

"You can't just walk up into my school and warn me not to go home. How are you even alive?"

Keelan and the girl exchange looks. Rather than two lovers sharing a bond, it is two people who know a secret forbidden to be told. None of them plan to explain to me how Keelan is here and in the flesh.

Keelan picks me up under my shoulders and lifts me from the ground. My heart pumps the adrenaline through my body, leaving me in shock and numb from the waist down. My legs wobble beneath me. I can't keep my balance. I sway back and forth.

"We have to leave now. They will be back," the blonde girl says.

"Who are you talking about? Those creatures that almost killed me?"

"The demons," she replies.

Keelan lifts my arms around his shoulder. Due to his height, I can hardly stand with my feet flat on the floor. He heads to the door and nods to the blonde behind him. I try to glance behind me, but he towers over me, blocking my view.

He leads me to an old black seventies Mercedes. The rusty door creaks as it opens. The seats are lined with ripped black leather, something straight out of a horror movie. But I don't hesitate to enter the car. After all that has happened, I don't care if I am being kidnapped or killed.

BOOM!

A shining light ignites the entire block. Fire explodes from above Keelan's silhouette. The head of the fire blows in like a desert storm. As I feel the heat of the fire on my face, I feel as if it has burned my eyebrows off. A terror convulse out of me like a patient in an asylum. I watch as the house I once knew goes up in flames. It crumbles and cracks into the soil.

Keelan pushes my legs into the car and slams the door. Everything is muffled. The ringing in my ears is dominant over my surroundings. The blonde girl comes running out of the burning house, untouched by the fire behind her. She leaps over the roof of the car and into the passenger seat with ease.

"We have got to go before they find her," Keelan cries.

"Who is coming?" I ask, but they both ignore me.

Keelan stomps on the pedal and I fly to the back window. My head misses the glass by inches. I crawl to the window beside me to catch one more glimpse of the corpse of a home. Its fire continues to burn with might. The memories of the past keep the fire alive and thriving. As the house gets smaller, I know my past was catching up to me and there was no way out.

I watch Keelan in the mirror. His eyes are dark and not his own. He is not the person I once knew. The Keelan I once knew would not fake his death, but even if he did, he must have done it for a good reason.

CHAPTER FIVE

My fingertips brush against the rough leather of the car interior. There's a small warm spot where I had laid. It is still dark outside, and there is no light other than from the full moon. There is no sign of the strange girl or Keelan.

I sit up. My head pounds and spins everywhere. My eyes have to adjust to the darkness. I see my breath in front of me. Fog is covering the windows, and wiping them makes the situation worse. Even though the doors are unlocked, I am still frightened to open them to see where I am. I don't know what could be lurking outside the car.

The door creaks and echoes around me. I cringe. A grove of trees surrounds me. They stand tall, but naked from the fallen leaves of fall. The branches twist and turn to block my view of the twinkling sky above. The wind is still. Nothing makes a sound. I am alone.

There are no keys in the ignition when I look in it. They left me with no way back and I'm not sure how far I am from town, or If I'm still in Massachusetts. I can't go back, anyway. Where would I go? There is no home left for me to return to. All that is left of it is ashes.

I somehow still have my phone in my pocket. I remember it being dead back at the house, and now, strangely, It has five percent left. It is just enough power to make a call. I have two bars; I have to take advantage of it.

Messages from Regina appear on my phone. Not one, but at least twenty messages and missed calls.

"Where are you?"

"Are you okay, Juliet?"

"There are fire trucks surrounding your house. Please tell me you are alive."

Without warning, I expel the contents of my stomach over a rock. It is mainly punch and alcohol. An unpleasant taste lingers in my mouth afterwards. My stomach cramps after dry heaving too many times.

Regina thinks I died. That means she left the dance and went to my house afterwards. Her house is in the opposite direction of the school. She wanted to see me, to see if I was alright. I can't even imagine her face when she saw the flames consuming my house. Did she think it was an accident? Or did she think I set my house on fire again? I can't come to a reasonable explanation.

Given my past, she is probably thinking the worst. Brody will find out and make up more rumors about me. Except, it would be about how I set my house on fire because I am completely insane; thinking Keelan was still alive.

Warm tears flood my eyes. How could I possibly be in this situation right now? I'd rather be in another psychiatric hospital than be here in the middle of who knows where.

"Hello?" I call out, my voice reverberating off the trees.

The trees rustle in the gentle flow of wind. I listen for a sign of anyone around me; a twig cracking or even someone crying. There is just nothing out there.

"Keelan, where are you?"

I walk a few feet away from the car, hoping to find someone, or a sign indicating where I am. I am lost, and I don't know how far I'd have to walk just to find a road or pay phone. I know if I go further into the dark forest, I'd surely be dead by morning. I have no chance of surviving the night.

I search the glove compartment and discover an assortment of paper documents, trash and a flashlight and conveniently a flashlight. I switch it on and a dim orange light comes through it. I wave in front of me, hoping to gain more light from it.

I refuse to stay here all night in this crisp, cold weather. I circle around trees and over rocks. I find nothing. I want to stop because I am so exhausted, but I'm in survival mode. The will inside me keeps me determined to find a way out.

I come across a tree with a dark liquid smeared across it. It was warm, so it is still fresh. As I look closer, I realize it was blood. It could be animal blood, or god forbid, human blood. I take a breath and continue on my path, following the trail of blood.

CRACK

The sound comes not from behind me, but in front of me. I shined the light in every direction. A dark horizon of trees goes on for miles. I'm only being paranoid. It's just an animal. *It is only an animal.*

In the distance, I hear crunching dirt and cracking twigs, but the sound seems to get louder. I shine the flashlight in every direction, looking for the source. Then the sound comes from behind me now. The flash light sputters. The batteries are almost dead. I hit it against my good hand to get it working again.

As the sound comes closer, the flashlight goes off and I am taken down to the cold ground. I am covered in cold dirt and grass. Something big laid on top of me, restricting my breathing. I try to push the being off, but it is too heavy for me to lift.

"Get off of me," I shout.

The being squirms off of me, and icy air fills my lungs.

I feel for the flashlight around me. I find the handle and scurry to grab it. The light sputters again but flips on with dim light. I see a bloodied man panting before me. He's hunched over trying to catch his breath.

"Who are you?" I ask.

"We have to get out of here. They are coming." the man pulls on my hand, but I snatch back from him.

"Who is coming?"

"I don't know. They attacked my wife out of nowhere. All I saw were glowing eyes," he breathes heavily with his hands on his head. He sobs. "What are you doing out here all alone?"

I don't answer his question, but I flash the light in every direction to get a clearer picture of what might be lurking in the shadows. All I see is the shadows of the trees shifting with the light. The man could be making up a sob story to lure me in. Or maybe his wife was taken by unknown beasts. How can I trust a lonesome man I had only just met?

In the distance, two round objects reflect at me. I squint, trying to see the figures in the dark. The man described seeing glowing objects before his wife was taken.

"Who's there?" I call.

Their eyes disappear and reappear in a matter of seconds. The glowing eyes of an animal look back at me. They become bigger as they trudge towards me. I am too shocked to move or run away. The eyes blink at me.

"We have to run, miss."

The man runs away from the glowing objects. The figure comes into the light of the flashlight. Only there isn't one, there are two.

"Keelan, is that you?"

"Juliet, what are you doing? Go back to the car," a low, raspy voice answers.

"I thought she would be out for hours. The drug didn't work on her," another voice says.

"Bristol. Go after him."

Bristol leaves in a flash after the man who trampled on me.

"What? What are you doing?"

"Juliet, he cannot know," Keelan says.

"Where are we? What is all over your face?" my hands tremble. "Did you kill that man's wife?"

As the screams travel through the air, I freeze. The man begins to whimper, and eventually there is complete silence. All my mind goes to is: *The man is dead. They killed that man.*

Keelan wipes something away from his face. His face differs from how it looked earlier. A wicked glow comes from his eyes, something like a cat's eye in the dark, and his mouth is red. Not red like from a rash, but red from blood, the blood from the tree.

I turn away, horrified by his appearance.

"Juliet, please don—"

"Don't what? Is that blood? Did you kill that man's wife?" My grip tightens around the flashlight. I tremble in his presence. *This can't be real.*

He holds his hand up to calm me, but with each step he takes forward, I take one backward. I rub my eyes, hoping this isn't real. But every time I look at him, the blood gets darker. My breathing becomes heavy and shortened. My chest is rising and dropping rapidly. I am dizzy; I am filled with so much energy. I want to scream.

Murderers have abducted me. Not just murderers, but my ghost friend that came back from the dead.

"Let me explain, please. Don't run," Keelan begs.

I shake my head. I can't rationalize with him now. Not after everything that has happened tonight.

"The blood. Did you...kill someone?" My voice shakes.

This is not Keelan. This is a cold blooded killer disguised as my old friend.

I look at the moon. Its brightness is in full effect. The energy of the moon surges within me. It isn't the rush of adrenaline; it is something more powerful. It is almost familiar. My fingertips tingle, and the sensation travels up my arms and to my chest. With every breath I take, the energy escalates. I realize I am at full power. I can release my power here if I want to. No one would know but me. The imposters will be dead within seconds.

"This is what you do? Am I your next victim? You are just like Regina and Brody." My voice projects off the trees like thunder.

"Juliet, stop. I would never hurt you. Please let me explain."

"No, I am done. You have invaded my life. I was healing from your loss. I thought I was better off without you"

Keelan's eyes drop. It finally clicks. He knows what he's done. Part of me regrets being so angry with him, but he has never once stopped to tell me why he has returned, or why any of this has happened. He's left me in the dark, literally. How could he be so careless? Enough to find him with blood on his lips.

I go into the dark place I vowed I'd never tap into again. It's in the back of my brain, where the darkest and oldest memories are held. The darkness I banished from my mind is slowly coming back. The information courses through my mind and soul. Every muscle and every ligament works harder than it ever has.

I hear my ancestors calling to me, and I hope one of them is my mother. I focus on their words. They whisper in my ear of dangerous things. I don't want to believe it. I blocked out their voices for so long now; I wonder how long they had tried to get me to listen to them. It all makes sense now.

"You didn't die in the fire."

Keelan cocks his head.

"You were dead even before I met you. This is the biggest secret yet." I laugh. "Funny, I'm a witch, and it took me this long to figure it out. I know why you had a closed casket funeral. Your body was never there."

Keelan and the girl glance at each other with the same look they gave each other hours ago. They know I caught him in his lie. There is no turning back now.

"You are the oldest creature to walk the earth. You are bloodsuckers."

I remember reading my mother's journals she passed to me. Countless information passed down from generations. In my mind,

I flip through every page ever read, and then I read them again. Her journals prepared me for this very moment. My magic is stronger than theirs. I can easily kill them in a split second and make it look like an accident.

"Bristol, you need to leave, now," Keelan demands. "She knows."

Keelan's pupils dilate. He doesn't look like himself anymore. He transforms into a sharp toothed, bloodthirsty monster. The veins around his eyes protrude, and they travel down his neck and into his arms.

The surrounding trees swirl in the wind. A branch cracks and falls to the ground beneath our feet. The wind twists through our hair in tangles. Cool air fills our lungs. This is my time. I know what I have to do, and I've known it all along. I only wish I had known it earlier.

I raise my palms to the moon. The energy electrifies my body. Every inch of the ground trembles beneath our feet, under my command. The feeling is euphoric. I have waited so long to release this kind of power. I can't hold it in any longer.

Keelan stands face to face with me now. His coal colored eyes penetrate my soul. I am angry, and I know he can sense it, too. I want to rip his heart out; I want to put every bit of energy I have into crushing him from the inside out, even if he is my best friend. He has kept the biggest secret from me.

"If you do magic, they will find you," he pleads.

The wind dies down drastically; the air is still cold. Without leaving my gaze, his fingertips find mine. The chills run through my body, and after the surge, my body returns to its resting state. My heart still races, but my muscles relax.

His fingers brush against mine. He takes my hand and lifts my arm to face level. As he observes the bloody sigil, his eyes become watery. His emotions are changing, making himself vulnerable. This is the Keelan I once knew; the one I missed most, but it is so hard to see him through his monster eyes.

"This was never supposed to happen." He continues looking at my hand, being careful not to cause me more pain than I am already in.

"They've marked you, and now you can't do magic without them finding you," he whispers. "You only set them back by using the holy water."

"Who are they? The people who gave me this?" I point to my arm.

His eyes meet mine, and he lowers my hand to his side.

"Please trust me when I say the man who gave you this cannot find you under any circumstance." His voice turns to a low tone, as if someone were watching us.

I snatch my hand away from him. It is difficult for me to piece all the information together. My body is covered in bruises and the pain is becoming unbearable. I'm still in my devil costume and I am freezing.

"How can I trust you? Are you even real?" I cry. I turn my body away from him, disgusted to be in his presence.

"Third period Algebra, sophomore year. It was a Tuesday. You had just found out that Bryan Leonard had chosen another girl over you. You spend most of the day in a foul mood. But during lunch, you had never laughed so hard in your life."

He remembers a day that we had both experienced together. It seems so long ago when it happened. He was right though; I was so upset, and I treated everyone, including him and Regina, so poorly. I was so angry. I don't know why he remembers that day, but no one else would have known but him.

He sounds promising, but maybe he is only lying to trick me. I want to trust him so much. After tonight, knowing what he is and what he is capable of is frightening. How can I trust him? He is my friend, or at least I thought so. I'm not sure anymore where we stand. For months, I thought he was dead. I grieved and finally thought I had found peace.

"Not only that, Juliet, but I know the truth behind your mother's death."

***

The grey sky sprinkles what seems to be ashes. I look far ahead and find no sight of a fire or smoke emerging from a volcano. The grass is burnt to a crisp; it crunches beneath my bare feet. The sky fills with smoke, and the air becomes dangerously hot.

This place should be familiar to me, but it isn't. I try to remember every place I have ever traveled to, and this is not one of them. The plain grasslands are a dull brown, but covered in ash from the sky. The horizon goes on for miles.

I am surrounded by headstones. Some have fallen over, and some are so worn the epitaphs are barely legible. I know I am in a cemetery, but as to which cemetery crosses my mind. I have only been to one in my life.

A chilling scream travels through the surrounding air. On the hill ahead of me, moving silhouettes dance in an eerie manner. I walk closer to it, hoping to get a better view. With each step I take, the hill moves further away from me.

The screaming becomes louder, and I am jolted forward a few feet from the scene.

"Hello, are you alright?" I ask.

The woman struggles on the ground, grasping her protruding stomach. I can't see her face, for it is blurry and distorted. I try to look for traces of blood on her stomach. The only blood I find is between her legs and pooled on the ground beneath her.

"I can help you." I scurry.

She can't hear me or see me. It's impossible for her to help herself. She flails her head around, screaming in constant pain. I attempt to touch her, but my hands fall right through her. There is no one around to call for help. I had never seen this type of magic. It's too late for me to save her.

I look between her legs and see a blood covered baby sprawled out on the ground. The helpless child screams in harmony with its mother. I struggle to look at both the mother and baby. The mother has yet to even look at her own child. She gasps for air.

The earth quakes, and the ground opens with a bright orange light. The heat grows with every opening. A man of a tall stature crawls up from the ground, untouched by the fire that swarms beneath him. He picks up the child in his arms and murmurs to it. He smiles wickedly and tosses the newborn into the pit of fire. He jumps in after the baby and the mother is no longer moving.

"No!" I lunged at the pit of fire.

Sweat rolls down my face as I sit up. The blinding light through the window wakes me from a deep sleep. A gentle breeze hits my face, and I become alert. I lay in a soft bed, with white sheets and blankets piled atop. The scent of lavender fills the room. A distressed vanity sits in the corner of the white room. Everything is so peaceful, but I am confused about how I got here.

I shift my body on the bed. An intense pain shoots through my arm. I look down and my arm is wrapped in gauze and medical wrap. Someone must have taken good care of my wound. My clothes differ from the night before. I am no longer wearing the devil costume. I'm dressed in a simple white t-shirt and grey pants. I cringe at the thought of someone seeing my body without me being awake.

I let my legs hang off the bed before I get up. Standing is a struggle, and every muscle in my body aches. My bones crack with every movement. I amin need of an aspirin and a pair of sunglasses. I truly feel like I am hungover.

A knock on the door rumbles through the room. I scurry to straighten my hair and wipe my face of the crust in my eyes.

"Uh, come in," I hesitate.

The door slowly opens, and a wrinkled woman shuffles into the room. Her cheeks sink into her face and her lips have no color. Her dress is a typical maid's uniform. It's certainly a sight to see, considering no one wears those uniforms anymore. There is no way she could be a vampire. She looks like death is right around the corner.

"Ms. Arden, you are invited to speak with Mr. Williams in the parlor," She croaks.

"Who is Mr. Williams?"

The woman sighs. "He is the owner of this house, ma'am. Arthur Williams."

She leaves the door wide open. Her feet slide against the wooden floors in the hallways. She is too old to even pick up her feet. She talks as if I am supposed to know who Arthur Williams was. I have never heard such a name in my entire life. Whoever brought me here are complete strangers.

I gaze out the dirty window. Dead trees surround me for as far as I can see. The grey sky is filled with dark clouds and migrating birds. The wind is still at the moment. I peek further down to the ground. I have to be at least three stories high. The paint is chipping off the siding, and dirt and leaves crumble into the windowsill. This place has to be as old as the vampires who live here.

Without hesitation, I exit the room. There is an instant change in the ambiance as I enter the hallway. It's dark, and the lanterns are dimly lit, giving off just enough light. The hallway is lined with a blue runner encased in years of dirt and dust. There are no windows in sight. The wallpaper peels off the wall. It's as if I have walked into a different timeline; back hundreds of years.

Down the winding staircase lines more lanterns. This is more Dracula's castle than a comfortable house. I am scared to descend into an unsteady staircase. Some steps are too loose for anyone to safely step on. I follow the scent of cedar. It gets stronger as I go deeper into the unknown.

From what I can see, there are countless closed doors. Any of which could hold Keelan, if he is even here. I want to investigate further into finding him, but I don't think it would be so easy to find him without being caught.

As I enter the lower level, I am met by an open living room. Old Victorian couches line the walls, and vintage rugs cover the entire square footage of the floors. Beneath the corner of the rug is a red stain. I wonder how much the original floor is covered in the red substance. I can't help but think it is blood splattered.

A chandelier hangs gracefully on the ceiling, and with any movement, it could shatter to the ground.

The smell of the cedar is strong in the area. I follow the runners to a door that is slightly ajar. The heat coming from the room is relieving. I knock lightly on the door. I hope so badly that Keelan is on the other side of this door.

"Come in, Juliet," a raspy voice answers. It definitely is not Keelan.

Pushing the door open, a grey cat perches on a table ledge to greet me. Its eyes are vibrant green, almost emerald like. The fur spreads out into a full winter coat. I reach out my hand to let it sniff me. It licks the tips of my fingers and it lets out a tiny sound.

The warmth is coming from a fireplace. Its aged structure is so intricate, and each design is unique in its own way. The shelf above the fireplace holds picture frames, none of which have one photo of Keelan in it. Maybe Keelan is not here, and he's only a mere transporter for a prisoner.

"I'm honored to finally meet you, the infamous Juliet Arden," the man chuckles.

His face is soft, not rough, like his voice suggests. I expected him to be dressed in an aristocratic vest and a tailcoat. Instead, he wears a simple button up grey shirt with dress pants. His accessories manifest his wealth; a silver pocket watch and nicely polished shoes. He appears too rich to be living in a musty, old home in the middle of nowhere.

"Arthur, I am assuming?" I stand by his chair.

He smirks at the informal greeting. He rises from the chair and tightens the cuffs on his wrist. I try not to stare, but he radiates with a pleasant personality and appearance. His dark hair slicks back behind his ears, reaching just below his shoulder line. His eyebrows are chiseled perfectly. How can someone so old be so beautiful?

"Nice to meet you. I hope Keelan's actions haven't affected you too badly." he shakes my hand with a strength that could easily break my hand. "I think it's time we get down to business."

"I want to see Keelan," I say.

His eyes focus on me, then the smile dissipates from his face.

"Keelan is unavailable."

"He is the only one I trust right now. I don't trust your kind." I cross my arms and squeeze myself for security.

Arthur is irritated. His demeanor changes when I mention Keelan. He turns to the bookshelf behind him and begins searching through the books. The silence is awkward, and I want to escape. But he has ears like a bat. Getting away is easier said than done.

"Why am I here? What is this place?" I beg.

He continues to look through the bookshelf, shuffling through each one thoroughly.

"This is your new home," he stammers. "Can you tell me about your dream?"

"How did you know about that?"

I think of the endless possibilities of how he could know about the dream I had this morning. It wouldn't surprise me if they had given me some drug to induce dreaming or have some type of mind reading ability. At this point, I'd believe anything. Hell, I'd even believe in fairies.

"We only gave you some herbal tea to help you sleep," He pauses, searching. "Mugwort can induce lucid dreaming."

That explains the terribly vivid dream I had this morning. There is a reason why I tend to stay away from mugwort. I had one bad experience, and I was done with it. I drank mugwort tea every day behind Edith's back. After a few days, my days and nights were getting mixed up, and I was confused about what was real and what wasn't. Never again, until now.

"What for? I'm tired of not getting any answers. No one is telling me anything," I cry.

He turns to me with his face buried in a book. He furiously flips through the pages. I stand impatiently, waiting for him to respond to my questions. I'm becoming so irritated. If what Keelan said was true about doing magic, I'd be defending myself alone from who knows what.

"I cannot give you too many details. But, read this, and you may find what you are looking for."

He hands me the book, but more or less chucks it into my hands. Hard leather lines the exterior of the book, the black is fading. There are no words on the front or back covers. I doubt this book can tell me why I had been attacked and kidnapped all in one night. I flip through the pages, stopping every few pages to read a few sentences. Most of the pages mention rituals, symbols, and demons.

Taking the book, I sit down near the fire to gaze at it for a little while longer. As I go further into the book, I come across more talk of demons, and even specific demons and their roles in hell. There is an abundance of different spells and rituals that all have the same comment written by it: **Summoned the wrong demon. Don't use this.**

This is dark magic. I'm trying to figure out why this kind of magic involves me. I've never performed a spell of this level ever in my life, nor would I ever have the thought of using it. This is the kind of magic that should be forbidden to all witches.

"What am I supposed to do with this?" I slam the book shut.

Dust goes flying in my face and covers my eyes.

"I cannot tell you why you are here, and why Keelan's actions have given him consequences."

What is that supposed to mean? Consequences? What could he have possibly done? Did he break rules, or even vampire laws? No one is being straightforward with me, and it angers me to the core.

"I forbid Keelan to talk to you any further." He situates himself in the chair by the fire.

"No. I deserve to know why I am here. Demons show up at my house and almost kill me, then my friend, who I thought was dead, shows up. Keelan is a vampire. Then I find out I am in a house of bloodsuckers. No, I need an explanation"

The door bursts open and cracks the wall behind it. Even with Arthur's excellent hearing, the sudden entry of Keelan startles him and I both. The lack of emotions spread across his face. He looks paler than ever, and his eyes are like two black holes sucking up the universe.

"Your mother is the one to blame."

CHAPTER SIX

Keelan stops me before I can reach him.

His hand goes up in a stopping motion. There is sorrow written all over his face. His pain radiates off of him, and me being a witch, I have mastered the art of reading people's pain and emotions. He wants nothing more than to be near me, and the magnetic pull is strong. I contemplate going to him. But something about Arthur's demeanor says it would be a terrible idea, not for me, but for Keelan.

"I know I'm not supposed to be here." He moves his body closer to the door, almost hiding behind it. "But you need to tell her the truth. All of it." He demands.

Arthur rubs the bridge of his nose. I can tell Keelan has caused problems before and Arthur is just sick of dealing with it. Keelan's eyes are serious, but he keeps his eyes on Arthur, as if to threaten him.

"Will one of you tell me what was going on?" I look back and forth between the two.

"Keelan, don't you dare say another word. The Elders are already angry with you." Arthur snaps.

Keelan mentioned my mother. How can she be part of this? She has been dead for eighteen years. I knew she was a very ambitious and cunning witch, and that was all my aunt had told me about her. I always suspected she was hiding more from me. Maybe I can finally find out the truth, even if it was from a bunch of bloodthirsty vampires.

"My mother, Esther, what about her? What did she do?" I ask.

Arthur's eyes penetrate Keelan. The room becomes uncomfortable, and the entire conversation is becoming awkward. Keelan has already said too much, but I want him to say more.

"Boy, you are no longer part of this mess you have made. You are in so much trouble as it is. The Elders will be here to see you any moment," he steps forward to Keelan as if he would lunge at him. "And I cannot protect you anymore than I have."

Keelan closes his eyes and sinks his head. His hands are in a ball. "She must know," He insists. "I took her away from all she had known. She needs to know."

"What must I know?" I yell.

"Your mother made a sacrifice to the devil. There, that is all I am saying," Keelan throws his hands into the air with defeat.

Arthur's eyes become blood red. "You foolish boy!" Arthur pins Keelan against the wall, and the sheetrock crumbles behind him. Keelan seems unsurprised by his lack of amusement on his face. He knew what was coming for him once he revealed more information.

"I am done saving you. Do you hear me, Keelan? I am done." Arthur squeezes Keelan's neck, but he is unaffected by the pain. The corner of his mouth twitches like he wants to smile, but stops himself.

A sudden and excruciating pain pulses through my arm. The pain becomes unbearable, and I fall to my knees. I hold my arm to my stomach, trying to breathe through the pain. I can feel the veins pulsing in my head. Keelan comes to my side and puts his hand around my shoulder. Arthur stands by, watching, unsure of what to do.

I can't help but cry out loud as tears cover my face. I am vulnerable. I don't feel safe. I want this pain to end. My stomach is turning. My hand is on fire and sizzles as if it has been dipped in acid; I can almost hear my skin popping.

"They are trying to locate her," Keelan shouts. "Arthur, do something."

Keelan rubs my back, trying to help me through the pain. His icy hands are soothing to my back, but he can't help the pain that travels down my arm.

Arthur isn't worried about what the mark was doing to me. He stands over me, ignoring my agony. His emotionless eyes penetrate through me. I try to keep myself from passing out, so I focus my view on Keelan.

"Do you trust me?" Keelan demands.

I can't think fast enough. Should I trust him? He's lied to me for years, and not over something small. He's one of them, and Arthur had made it clear he's not my friend. How can I trust the boy who faked his death? How can I trust him when he left me to grieve his death? He is still the boy I once knew. Somewhere inside of him, the old him is there.

"Juliet, do you trust me?"

"Yes, I trust you," I stutter. I wobble back and forth. The pain is not subsiding, but escalating with every breath I take.

"Please forgive me."

***

As I scramble up from the couch, I regret it immediately. My head pounds endlessly. Keelan kneels by my side, and eyes filled with sympathy. He soaks a cloth into a basin of water and pats it on my forehead. The pain is no longer in my hand, but in my head. I graze my fingertips across the cut over my eyebrow.

"You hit me with a lamp," I cry.

"I had to. They were trying to track you. They can't track your conscious mind," Keelan sniffs.

He rinses the cloth in the bloody water. I watch the blood release in the water like fog. His eyes turn black, and the look of a beast consumes him. His breathing is heavy. The smell of the blood bothers him. I don't know how he could go this long without showing his true side. How can a vampire hide the killer side of themselves without being caught?

"Are you okay?" I ask. I watch his every move. I still don't fully trust him. I'm ready to defend myself if I have to.

"Why are you asking if I am okay? I hit you with a lamp." He avoids eye contact with me.

"The blood."

"I can control myself just fine." He leaves the cloth in the basin and applies a bandage to my head.

He resumes his position by my side. I relax and let my back rest on the arm of the chair. He observes his hands. The blood dries on his skin. The both of us, short of words. I don't know what to say to make anything better. The damage is already done. We both are hurting.

I caress his cheek. He winces at the touch but does not remove my hand. By the way he shuts his eyes, he enjoys the warmth of my hand against his cold skin. His skin is cold, but I don't remember it being this cold before he faked his death. The feeling is almost unreal. I feel like it is too good to be true. How can he be here? Part of me still believes I am living in a nightmare.

His hand meets the back of mine. "I'm so sorry for everything. I'm sorry for bringing you into this mess. All I wanted was to protect you."

He positions his hand down by his side, but I continue to hold it. I want to hold his hand forever.

"I grieved your loss for months. I thought you were dead. Everyone did. Do you understand how broken I was?"

He lowers his face. Tears threaten to appear, and my voice becomes shaky. I take a breath.

"The scars on my face are a constant reminder of you, and I have to live with that every day." I situate myself on the couch to stop myself from getting emotional. I feel like I have cried too much in the past year. There has to be an end to it.

"Keelan, the kids at school, they called me a murderer. Not only that, but Brody started that rumor."

Anger rises in his face, and a single tear forms in the corner of his eye. His eyes turn black and red with fury. The veins in his face turn purple and travel down his neck. His energy shifts from sadness to rage.

"I'm going to kill him," he growls.

"No," I shout. "It doesn't matter now. What matters is you telling me, what the hell is going on?"

His lips quiver. With his eyes closed, he inhales and exhales slowly, breathing through the anger and hunger. He calms himself to where he is no longer a threat to me or himself. It's frightening how fast he can flip a switch and become a monster, but even faster to tame the demon inside him. The constant switch of emotions isn't normal. I can't imagine going from one feeling to the next. I would feel completely out of my body.

"I disobeyed orders. I was told to not get close to you. I let myself in and I will never regret that. The only thing I am sorry for was letting it go this far to where your life is in danger," He trembles.

I retract my hand from his and rest it on my lap. I run my thumb against the burn mark on my arm. It is numb at the moment, but the sight of it makes my stomach turn.

"I've been alive for many years, Juliet. I was always told that this would happen one day. They trained me to protect you. The one thing I wished was that you are never the one I had to protect."

I understand what he did. What a cruel and daunting task. To protect someone you may fall in love with. I can never imagine that kind of heartbreak. Knowing that person may live or die. But why would he want to protect someone he couldn't have a life with? He must have had no choice.

He stood by me countless times when I cried over stupid boys. He comforted me when I had my heart broken by the ignorant. It hurt him watching me love another when all he wanted was for me to give him that same affection. He watched my lips kiss another's. Part of me always knew how he felt about me; I was always blind to the truth.

"You don't know how much I've missed you. " I whisper.

His eyes meet with mine, and in this moment I can truly see who he is. I see a different side of him. He has opened himself up to me, something he would have never done back in school. He is an entirely different person. Knowing my fate must have made him more distant. But even that didn't stop him.

"I've missed you too."

The door jolts open, and a breeze follows

"Bristol. What do you want?" Keelan sighs.

"Arthur would like a word with Keelan."

In the room's light, her platinum blonde hair shines. Her piercing blue eyes sparkle at me. Her entire demeanor screams *mean girl,* but I have yet to know who she is, or how old she is. If she is anything like her father, intimidating and careless. I don't want to set her off.

Bristol stands in the doorway, eyes glistening with distress. Somehow, Keelan has a hunch of what is going on. It takes only a look from Bristol, and Keelan knows what is about to go down. The way they communicate by simply looking at each other makes me believe they have some sort of mind-reading capability.

Keelan and I remain speechless. I wait for him to inform me of what's going on. I throw the blanket off of me and onto the floor. Keelan looks at me, confused, as if I had disrespected the blanket.

"You aren't going anywhere," he commands. He grabs my hand as I head for the door, making me trip.

I jerk my hand away from him. His strength actually surprises me. I rub my wrist and fully observe the redness that surrounds it. A bruise will be noticeable by morning.

"You can't always protect me. Whatever is going on, it involves me now."

He knows I am right. The look of defeat spreads across his face. He realizes I am no longer the shy and sensitive girl I used to be. He can't boss me around like a puppy. He brought me here for whatever reason. For all I know, he could have just wanted to leave me to die. I don't understand why he doesn't realize that I am here for a reason.

"You are staying here. If I have to hit you with a lamp again, I will not hesitate," he growls.

The way he asserts himself leaves me speechless. His eyes become blackened with hatred and guilt. The eyes of a beast consume him. He snarls at me like I am his prey. I back down, slightly taken aback by his behavior.

He leaves the room hastily. The door's slam echoes in the tiny room. It's quiet now. I can't hear the creaking of the stairs.

I can tell by the way Bristol and Keelan looked at each other, something bad is about to happen. Keelan left without saying goodbye, and Bristol followed behind him, slamming the door. I heard them talk of the elders earlier, but I have no thought of who they could be. Leaders of the vampires of some sort.

I put my ear to the door and listen for any sound. All I can hear is the feet shuffling on the hardwood floor below. Hard floors run throughout the house, and there's nothing inside the walls to absorb the sounds. Every little noise can easily be heard by prying ears like mine.

"You disobeyed the clan's orders, Mr. Harrington," a smooth voice shouts.

"We must punish you for your behavior. This goes against everything we have told you"

Much more is heard, but most is muffled talking. They seem to argue. I can't hear Keelan's voice in the conversation.

"She is here? You ignorant bastards."

"You have risked the Sanguinem Luna clan from exposure."

Sanguinem Luna? Must be the clan's name. Such an odd name to name a vampire clan. It translates into blood moon. Very fitting, considering they drink blood to survive and only come out at night. Although I find it interesting Keelan has been able to walk in the light the entire time I have known him. There has to be a way around that.

"Death…. Cut off your blood supply for a century."

Oh no. They are talking about Keelan's punishment. I can't let this go down. I have to do something. I can't be the cause of death for someone who tried to save me. Keelan is my best friend, always will be mortal or immortal. I can't let them go through with this.

"Can't we just kill the girl?"

I back away from the door, careful not to make any loud noises, fearing they may hear me eavesdropping.They seriously can't think killing me would be a good idea. All they would do is huddle around my dead body and drain me of my blood. Who's to say Keelan wouldn't join in as well? I have to get out of here. I don't care if I didn't know the complete story. I will not stay to read the end.

I search around the room for ways to escape. I could kill myself and remove myself from this mess. No, too permanent. The dusty window seems like a good place to start. I look down into the grass below the bedroom. I have to be at least two stories up, but the roof slants just enough so I might slide my way down and levitate myself from hitting the ground.

I stop and listen to the conversation. I hear nothing but the breath inside my lungs. I look down at the scene surrounding the house. Trees surround the mansion for miles, and it seems it is the only house in the area. If I leave, who's to say where I might end up or who I'd run into.

I gulp and cautiously slide the window up. It's quiet, but I still cringe with each pull. The chilly breeze hits my face with a blast. I've only got a shirt on and sweatpants. Not anywhere near enough clothing to keep me warm. But the cold weather is a better option than staying here a minute longer.

Left foot. Right foot over the windowsill. I regret escaping this way when a cold burst of wind blew over me and almost knocked me down the side of the roof. I catch myself in the gutter. I hang there like a bat. I can't pull myself up, but I know better. I am a witch, for god's sake. I know spells to make myself silent.

Keelan told me not to use magic, but I don't care at this point. I'll do anything to escape this prison guarded by vampires. I will not let their rules intimidate me. Their strength cannot keep me here.

"Corpus levitate."

My body becomes weightless, and I let go of the gutter one finger at a time. I am floating in midair. It's a rush to be weightless and powerful at the same time. The last time I tried this spell was a month before the accident. I did it while the sky was black and the stars shined so bright. I felt so close I could almost touch them. It would be amazing to fly so high that I could see the horizon and the curvature of the earth.

"Descendit"

My feet float above the ground. The weight sinks as my feet touch the ground. I catch my balance. I search around for any way of transportation. There is nothing insightful except an old wheelbarrow and a small worn down shed next to the house, not big enough for what I am looking for.

I guess running is my best choice. After sprinting towards the trees, I don't look back. The last thing I want is for anyone to follow me. I doubt I even got away as quietly as I did. A vampire's hearing is nothing but deadly. If they can hear a heart pumping blood, then they can even hear an ant carry dirt.

I run through the forest of dead trees, each with their own barrier of fallen limbs and twigs standing out. I dodge and roll on the ground to avoid any further obstacles. I never look back to see how far I have gone. I am going to keep running till I can't anymore, even if it damn near kills me.

As I am running, I find myself with a mouth full of dead leaves. I don't remember a branch on the path. After spitting out the crumbled leaves, I did my best to get dust off.

"What the hell."

"Sorry about that," a boy emerges from the trees. "Ms. Arden, isn't it?"

Nodding my head, I watch him like a hawk as he inches closer to me. He has a similar appearance to Bristol, an all too similar look alike. They have the same crystal blonde hair and blue eyes.

"Forgive me, I am Allister Williams."

"Bristol's brother?" I interrupt.

He smiles. "Twin, actually. Although I never thought we looked alike much."

He fiddles with the contraption in his hands.

"Where are you going, if I might ask?" His accent confuses me, for he talks too fast for my brain to comprehend his words.

"I was just taking a jog... through the forest." I lie.

Why would I lie to a vampire? I am so stupid.

"Isn't it great? Not a single town for miles from here and blocked off from society. I just love how quiet it is," he laughs.

He catches me in the lie. I am scared he might drain me of my blood, or even far worse, take me back to that wretched house. Although the air was getting colder every second, I'd rather be stranded in this forest than with any blood sucker.

"You could have just listened to Keelan's warning and maybe you wouldn't be in this mess." He circles around me, looking me up and down as if to take a bite out of me. I swear I can see drool in the corner of his mouth.

"So you are the girl Keelan was supposed to keep alive?" He looks me up and down and scoffs.

"What was that, in your hand?" I ask.

He turns and scratches at the metal looking box. He shakes it a few times, hoping to hear something inside. Nothing rattles.

"Pandora's box," he says. "Nothing to worry about, though. Only a god can open it. I am studying its magical properties. It's hard to come across something like this in a lifetime."

He sits the box down like it was nothing, and if it was what he said it was, then I'd steer far away from that thing. Who knows what was lurking inside of it. How did he even get his hands on such an ancient and deadly artifact? But maybe he's lying and only trying to scare me.

"Can you tell me what was going on?"

"No," He sighs. "But I can give you some advice."

I feel his icy breath flow over my cheek as he comes inches from my face.

"If you can't do magic, have someone do it for you."

He walks away and returns to the box. He shakes it a few more times.

"I can do that? But I don't know anyone who could help me. I don't know another witch who is alive."

He laughs once more. It seems all he knows how to do is laugh at my silly questions.

"If I could have it my way, I'd kill you just so this nonsense would go away."

His words send chills down my spine. I've never met someone so abnormal, except maybe my aunt, but she is at least human. As wicked as she is, I'd rather be around her than this cryptic vampire. I feel sorry for the unlucky few who were consumed by him. He seems like the type of vampire to have no remorse for murdering innocent people. I could never live with myself if that ever happened to me.

"You really think you can run from us, huh?" A voice calls back.

I draw my attention to Bristol, who is standing right behind me.

"You can't run, Juliet. We are vampires. We hunt. I can smell you from a mile away," She flips her hair. "Besides, you have nothing and no one to go back to."

In my mind, I see my home burning to the ground. Regina thinks I'm dead, Edith probably thinks the same too. I still don't know why she wasn't there when I came home. Maybe she knew the demons were coming. How could she leave me to fend for myself? How could she be that willing to just get rid of me like that? To the outside world, I no longer existed. My life as I know it is no more. It's like I'm already dead.

I'm tempted to keep running, but it's a stupid idea considering she found me in a small amount of time. I would never make it, and I would never survive the cold. My human body cannot tolerate the cold like the vampires can.

"Listen, Keelan was in trouble the moment you became friends, leaving now won't help him or anyone."

She is right. I care about Keelan too much to cause him any more pain. I'm not sure if I will ever see him again. But knowing he may still be alive while I return may be the best thing for all of us.

"You must go," Allister says.

I turn to face him, and he is nowhere to be seen. The box is also missing. Bristol stands by me with her arms crossed.

"He is very... dramatic," I say.

Bristol chuckles quietly.

"Finally, someone agrees with me."

We walk through the field that separates the house from the trees. Bristol hovers over me, ready to take me down if I so much as flinch. I can't outrun her, but I doubt my abilities because I was able to escape from the second story floor. I pride myself in that one accomplishment.

We enter the house and everything is quiet until Artur comes stomping around the corner of the parlor.

"How did she escape?" He yells.

Arthur grabs a hold of my wrist, the same one that Keelan pulled on earlier. At the end of the night, I might have a broken wrist.

Bristol backs away from her father with scared eyes.

"Did you use magic?" He breathes. " Is that how you escaped?"

"Why does it matter to any of you if I use magic or not? If the demons are truly after me, I'd rather be killed by them than live here another minute."

Keelan walks around the corner with his head down. The Elders follow behind him, as if to guide him to another room.

"Keelan, what is going on?" I scream.

"You are never to speak to Keelan again. Is that clear?" Arthur blocks me from Keelan.

Bristol leaves my side and retreats up the stairs. Arthur still has a firm grip around my wrist. He pulls me away from the entrance and through the kitchen, where we are met with a tall, white door. He opens it, almost hitting the wall behind it. We step on old wooden stairs as we descend into the cellar. I cannot see a thing.

"Where are you taking me?"

"Somewhere you can't cause any more damage."

He releases me, and I'm thrown to a cold and wet floor. I'm still unable to see what is in front of me. I don't know where I am. All I know is, this is no place for a human.

There are heavy footsteps around me, and chains clatter above me. Soon, both of my arms are above my head and metal cuffs are strapped onto my wrists. The weight of the cuffs make it impossible to hold them up.

"What are you doing?" I cry. "You can't keep me here forever."

Moments later, I hear what sounds to be like a rusted metal door shut. I try to lift myself from the ground, but the chains are too heavy to move any farther. I pull on them with everything I have in me. The rust of the cuffs scrape against my skin, making my skin feel like it's on fire.

"You will be safe here."

I hear the muffled sound of the creaking wooden stairs, but it gets quieter and quieter till I can't hear anything but the beating of my own heart. My chest fills with sorrow, and it feels like everything has been drained from my chest cavity. It is almost empty.

How many times in one night can a girl be kidnapped? No one knows I'm still alive. Everyone thinks I'm dead because my house was set on fire. No one knows the truth. I will never be saved. I'm in a house with a bunch of bloodsuckers who are holding me captive, and none of them are telling me anything.

Do I pray?

Who do I pray to?

I'm going to starve to death down here. I can't even remember the last time that I ate. My body is going to slowly shut down. I'll stop breathing, then my heart will stop, and every other organ will follow. I will fade into nothing. It won't be a fast and painless death. Everything will happen so slowly. Then, right when I'm about to die, all of the vampires and their friends will feed on me.

CHAPTER SEVEN

The water dripping on the wet stone repeats in my mind. It's always the same consistency, and always the same tone. Over and over it drips. I don't know where the water is going, or if it will ever stop. All I hear is the loneliness that consumes me. It sends me into a state of insanity.

I don't know how much time has passed since Arthur shackled me down here. Hours could have passed, maybe even days. Time passes while I rot down here. No one has even once been down to check on me. Not even Keelan.

If I miraculously live through the torment, I'll stop at nothing to uncover the truth. Not just about Keelan, but about my entire life. Keelan said my mother was part of this, and I try to form every possibility of what that might mean. Nothing makes sense.

It hurts to move my muscles. My fingertips brush against the mark on my arm, it is scabbing over. It feels rough and almost swollen, like it's infected. I could easily die of sepsis if the burn is left untreated. Who knows what ancient creatures could be lurking down here, waiting to enter my body.

"Juliet, come on we have to go."

Keelan's voice rings through my ears. It's almost as if he is standing right next to me. My ears may be playing tricks on me again. What could they have done to me this time?

One arm falls to my side and my injured hand hangs in the air. I try to pull it down, but it's somehow still connected to the wall.

"Hold on, I got you."

I feel cold hands run down my arms, shaking me to full consciousness. Suddenly, both hands are by my side now, numb and motionless.

My brain clicks. Someone is in the room with me. *Keelan.*

"Keelan. What's going on?"

He pulls me up to my knees. My head slouches forward. I am too weak to hold my body on my own.

"We have to get you out of here before they come back," He says.

"Before who comes back?"

"Arthur and the others. They left."

My head is spinning. All the blood is rushing to my head and I can barely see straight. My legs become wobbly beneath me. I'm giving it my all to walk just a few feet away. My knees buckle and I go toppling forward. Keelan catches me inches away from hitting my head on the ground.

"I am so sorry I let this happen to you. I didn't want this."

I hear the sincerity in his voice. Despite being unable to see him, I feel the emotion in his words. I am too weak to respond. My vocal chords feel like they have been stripped of every muscle that makes them work. My hands are on his shoulders and I let him lead the way up the stairs.

The brightness from the kitchen blinds me. Keelan stands in front of me with his hands on my shoulders.

"Are you okay?" He asks.

I nod.

"We have to get you something to eat, and then we have to go somewhere that Arthur and the Elders won't find you," Keelan sits me at the small table in the corner. "Hold on, I'll be right back."

Keelan disappears around the corner. I watch him to make sure he is completely out of the room. I lift myself up quietly, wincing with every move I make.

I enter the hallway and shuffle towards the parlor where I first met Arthur. I want to look through the endless amount of books he has lined against the wall. There has to be at least one book that will tell me more about my mother, since they seem to know all about what she did. I am determined to find out, even if it kills me.

Thinking back to my dream, I try to deconstruct each part of my dream, starting with the woman I saw. Flashes of the bloody baby cross my mind, but I try to shake it out of view. A tall man took the baby and threw it into the fire. The more I dig deeper into this, the more I'm scared to say what it is out loud.

Sacrifice. That is what I gathered from Keelan and my dream. My mother had to have been in a sacrificial ritual. I wouldn't believe it at first, but even her old journals that my aunt kept suggested she was into dark magic at one point. Her book talked about demons and hell. I still can't wrap my head around something like it. She had to have been desperate to perform dangerous forms of magic.

Why would she sacrifice someone, especially a baby? Did she have a baby before me and thought sacrificing that child would be a good idea? What was she trying to gain from it? It could be money, fame or even worse things like power. My Aunt would be of no help. I know she never approved of my mother and her witchcraft.

The questions are eating at me from the inside out. I want to call Edith desperately, but I'm not sure where I would even start. "Hey, I'm still alive. Keelan isn't dead, he's a vampire, and I'm being held hostage, come save me." The scenario is ridiculous.

"Ms. Arden, is everything alright?" A scratchy voice calls behind me.

"Oh yes, I'm just looking for something to read," I smile, hoping she would ask no further questions.

"Would you like some tea?"

"Yes, please."

She turns with her duster in hand and scuttles down the hallway. Such a pleasant woman. I had a feeling they may have drugged her. She doesn't seem bothered by living in a house of vampires. She may not even know what is going on. No one could willingly want to live here.

I search the top shelves closest to the door. Everything is in alphabetical order and color coded. Most of these books are history books from all ages, including the Golden Age. Some books are older than others, some are worn and some are unreadable.

I only had a short amount of time before Keelan would return, or worse, Arthur and his clan. I search fast and as thoroughly as I can without missing a single title.

The next section is more of vampire lore and history, something I'm not interested in. I know everything I need to know about those blood suckers. For centuries they live, traveling from place to place, killing people along the way just to survive. Their blood lust sickens me. I know it's something they can't control, but If I ever became one of them, I'd kill myself. I couldn't live with the fact that I would have to kill to live.

A shelf full of leather bound journals catch my attention. Any of them have to be Keelan's. I want to know more about his life and where he came from. He is so closed off he rarely showed emotion, but when he did, it was intense.

I pick one journal, whose leather spine has been scratched. The brown is fading around the edges. A red ribbon pokes out at the bottom. I open it; it belongs to Arthur. I turn it to the page where the bookmark sits. Seeing as how I am snooping, I'm not sure if I should have read them, but if no one is going to be honest with me, I have to find out the truth myself.

November, 10th, 1979

Throughout my many years of existence, I have never met someone so spectacular. She was exquisite in every way. Her very being warms my cold blood. I want nothing more than to be with this woman for the rest of eternity. Victoria Mason, love of my life. Her beauty exceeds the rest. I live to see her every day. Her smile was like nothing I have ever seen before.

Her magic was incredibly powerful. She was very talented in the light and dark arts. For many years I have searched for someone with such power. She was by far the most beautiful and knowledgeable witch ever to live.

I am deeply saddened. I must leave her. The Sanguinem Luna clan has become part of something very dangerous. I musnt say a word to her, I must leave immediately. It breaks my heart into a thousand pieces. I wonder if our souls will ever meet again. Till then, I love you, dear Victoria Mason.

My heart breaks into a million pieces. The man I had met a few days ago seemed so emotionally cut off. The centuries old man found the love of his life. He loved this woman, Victoria Mason, and something happened where he could no longer be a part of her life. I can only imagine the years of heartbreak he endured.

Victoria Mason is a witch. She might still be alive now, I'm not sure. She had to have been young in nineteen seventy-nine. Surely she would have been in her sixties by now. It's possible she may still be alive. I may get my hopes up, but I have to start somewhere.

I tuck the journal under my arm and tiptoe back to the kitchen. When I enter, Keelan stands in the doorway with his arms crossed. I peer to the table beside him. There is a full plate of steaming food..

"What's that you got there?" He asks. By the way he stands, he already knew where I was. It's the vampire hearing.

"Just an old book."

He reaches out for it, but I turn away quicker than he can grab it. A smile crosses his face for a split second, then returns to his stern look.

"I could hear you in the parlor, Juliet. What book is that."

I hesitate, but I hold out the old journal.

"This is Arthurs. He spared your life once. I don't think he will be so kind again," he holds it in his hand, hesitant to look through it. "Besides, we rarely have guests that snoop. Not even I have the audacity to rummage through his belongings."

He takes the book near the window and flips through the pages. His eyes are shaking through the pages of journal entries. He, too, is mesmerized by Arthur's life. Arthur probably never divulges his darkest secrets to anyone, not even his own children. These aren't just secrets, these journal entries were about love.

"There was a woman Arthur used to know, Victoria Mason," I step to him, but he takes one step back. "She's a witch. If I could just find her."

"She was here a day before you arrived."

My heart skips a beat, making me gasp for air. The butterfly sensation fills my belly. Finally, I feel like I am getting somewhere.

"She's alive." I mutter.

Keelan slams the book shut and forcefully gives it back to me. He doesn't want to take any part in the secrecy.

"You must know, there are things in there that," He inhales. "kind of predict the future."

"Is it about me?" I shake.

He nods.

I inhale quickly. I wait for him to continue the conversation, but clearly it isn't happening.

"If that is true then, will you help me?" I ask.

He rubs his eyes.

"I can't."

"You can help me get out of here. Where does Victoria Mason live?"

"I don't know," He pauses. "But I know she works at a nightclub in the nearest city."

"Great! You're going to take me to her." I head for the door once more.

"Juliet, wait," I let go of the doorknob. "You must know something. I have broken many laws for you. I should be dead like, really dead. If I help you, it may cost us both of our lives."

Goosebumps form on my arms. An eerie tingle strikes down my back. Deep down, I know this is a bad idea for the both of us, but if Satan is really after me, he will stop at nothing to find me. So either way, I am dead.

"If you go down, I go down with you."

***

Arthur and his have yet to come back home. Thank God, because I don't want to see Arthur's wrath when he comes back to find me not in the cellar anymore. That terrifies me more than sneaking away to find Arthur's past lover.

We come across the black Mercedes he picked me up with on the night of the dance. It's covered in a camouflage tarp and faux leaves, easily hidden in the bushes from anyone venturing too far.

"How are you able to hide this from Arthur?" I ask as I enter the car.

"Arthur rarely leaves the house. He travels on foot most of the time. He never comes out here."

"What about Bristol and Allister? Wouldn't they tell him?" He starts the car with a rumble.

"We all share this car."

It sounds like they're a bunch of rebellious teenagers, sneaking out so the big and bad father doesn't catch them. Except they aren't teenagers, they are adults in a teenager's body. Seems like a great idea, hiding the car from an old and powerful vampire. I chuckle to myself. I guess vampires had to have fun, too.

I lay the journal on my lap. Keelan pays no attention to its existence. I want to read further into it, but I fear doing so would only put me at more risk. I can't know too much. I can't have them looking into my mind and seeing all the knowledge they fought so hard to hide.

We drive through trees for what seems like forever, but there is a small path he follows. He must have been this way thousands of times. He knew every turn and rock on the trail. He could probably drive blind if he wanted to.

The tires skid as we enter the main road. I want to roll the window down and stick my head out like a dog and enjoy the cool breeze of the winter air. I don't want to embarrass myself. I am already on thin ice with Keelan. I can't mess it up.

I drift off to sleep too many times. Each time I wake up, we are still on the road. I don't know how far we have gone, or how close we are to our destination. Keelan is still driving with his hands gripped tightly around the steering wheel. I wish I knew what he was thinking. Is he mad at me? Does he want to tell me things he knew he shouldn't?

I don't want to be the one to break the silence. I know I have already caused too much trouble for the both of us. I can tell by the way the corner of his mouth twitches. He wants to say something.

If only he would just let his fears say what's on his mind. This is hard for the both of us. The secrets we both hold keep us apart, and I don't know how to mend our relationship back together. If it could be fixed.

I see buildings of every size and color. Most of them look familiar, but it's unclear because of the darkness and blaring lights around us. The amount of cars doubled in the past hour or two. Cars speed past us and swerve in front of us like they had somewhere to be. We have finally made it onto a major highway.

"Salem. We're in Salem," I yawn.

He broke out of his trance and straightened his back.

"Oh yeah. How did you know?"

I crease my eyebrows in frustration.

"We went on a field trip to a museum here once. Don't you remember?" I beg.

"Yeah, yeah, of course. Lots of fun." He remains expressionless.

I doubt he remembers the field trip. His dull eyes concentrate on the road ahead.

"I broke my ankle walking down the museum steps. It wasn't so fun."

He mutters something under his breath. He really forgot about the trip, or maybe he isn't paying attention to what I'm saying. I hope he didn't forget the most treasured memories we both share. I know there is so much going through his mind, but I can't imagine what I would do if he completely erased our memories. How could I talk to him if his memories aren't there anymore? Is he really the Keelan I once knew, or has someone taken over his mind?

We speed past the tall historical buildings. They are beautiful and unique in every way. I find it funny we ended up in Salem, home of the witch trials in the sixteen hundreds. I feel the energy of every witch ever hung and burned on the stake. The energy manifests itself as a caffeine high, a pleasant feeling, yet it is very new to me.

"Did you witness the trials?" I ask, hoping he is listening.

"I'm not that old," he chuckles. "Do I look that old to you?"

That's a rather sarcastic question to ask. Vampires don't age.

We turn down a street that is brightly lit. People of all kinds walk the streets with smiles on their faces. They have colorful drinks in one hand and cigarettes in the other. Some girls stumble over their feet while their friends catch them in laughter. What truly makes me jealous is the joy on their faces. They have no worries. Life seems great for them. Oh, how I wish I had a normal life. Instead, I have the ruler of hell after me.

I've always wanted to see more of Salem, but not the nightlife part of it. I want to see more of the history and the sites of where the witches were hung. I want to see the church where the witches stood on trial, waiting to hear if they were guilty or not. During the field trip, we only had the chance to visit the museum, but it never went into the very specifics I am interested in.

We come to the brightest building on the block. Neon lights ignite the block to get people's attention to lure them in. People line up near the door and it extends down the sidewalk to the stop sign. The music is loud and can be heard from the outside. The vibrations rattle my head uncomfortably.

While I admire the building's architecture, Keelan meets me to open the door. I hadn't seen him leave the driver's side, let alone turn the car off. He holds his hand out like a perfect gentleman. It is a better act than when he pushed me into the car after he blew my house up.

"So, how are we going to get in?" I ask.

I scratch my hand where the mark is. I had forgotten about it. I pull my sleeve over my hand, hoping to hide it from the other's around me. But something told me the alcohol would make them oblivious to any mark on my skin.

"This way." Keelan gestures.

I follow behind him to the front entrance. A bald man with muscular arms stands guard in the doorway, bobbing his head to the music. His black bandana covers his forehead, stopping the sweat from dripping into his eyes. He appears almost statuesque.

"Keelan Harrington," He says to the man.

The bald man peers behind Keelan and eyes me curiously.

"And the girl?"

"She is twenty-one. She is with me."

Keelan speaks confidently as if he has been here a million times. He must have come here many times while still attending school. He easily passes for a twenty-year-old. His name is clearly on the VIP list. There is so much he isn't telling, and I know I'm going to pull it out of him in one way or another.

Keelan enters the club with me trotting behind him like a groupie. I look ridiculous in my casual wear. I didn't have time to prepare to look like I actually fit in here. I am standing out like a sore thumb. I'm surprised there isn't some type of dress code. My casual wear wouldn't cut it.

"How many times have you been here exactly?" I yell from behind him.

"Don't worry about it." He raises his hand as if to hush me.

People are dancing to the beat of the music; drink in hand and bodies grinding. The lights flashed white and green. Intricate chandeliers hang gracefully from the ceiling. People sit at the tables surrounding the dance floor, eating and drinking. Towards the back, a group of white older men sit in a booth smoking cigars with beautiful women on their hips.

We stand by the bar. I look around, but I'm not sure who to look for. I have never seen Victoria in my life, let alone knew she existed. Is she older? What is she wearing? Is she a hippie? If she works at a nightclub, I half expected her to dress like a younger person, but look older. Like she is trying to be something she isn't.

Witches are able to use anti aging spells. You could be damn near one hundred years old and still look like a forty-year-old. It doesn't stop aging completely, but heavily slows it down. I don't know if Victoria used that spell or not. So it's hard to say if im looking for a younger or older woman,

"There." Keelan points. I follow his finger to the main stage, where a woman is standing in front of DJ equipment. She has big headphones over her ears. Below her, she plays with the controls. She moves to the music with a smile on her face. Surely she can't be the Victoria that Arthur was referring to in his letter.

"That's Victoria? We have to talk to her."

"No. She isn't so kind to people who demand her attention," Keelan stops me.

"So we have to wait till she's done?"

"Mhm."

My first impression of her has already gone down the drain. The way Keelan describes her sounds like she doesn't want to be bothered. I'm nervous to meet her now. What if she turns me down? What if she won't give me the time of day? I try to push off the social anxiety. I'm here for a reason and one only. I have to convince her to help me.

One thing I do know. She looks about twenty-five. It is likely she used the aging spell. She is beautiful. I have to know why she wanted to use the spell in the first place.

We sit at a table next to the bar. Servers come up to us, but Keelan waves them away each time. I can't help but think Keelan doesn't want to talk to me, or even want me here. I know he probably thinks he has already said too much, but now isn't the time to hold back. His silence is deafening.

"Can we at least go dance?" I gently tap his arm. "I'm getting bored watching people make a fool of themselves."

He looks at me as if I'm not thinking clearly. I mean, maybe that is true, but I'm only trying to get him to open up to me. If we have to wait to talk to Victoria, he might as well entertain me. Besides, he owes it to me. He set my house on fire.

"No. Not a good idea," He shakes his head.

"I've endured enough these past few days. I need to do something fun for once."

His gaze pierces my eyes. I can see his mind going in all sorts of directions. He wants to say no, but his heart is telling him yes.

"Fine." He stands up and holds out his hand like earlier.

I follow him to the middle of the dance floor. People haven't noticed we are there. It's great not to be noticed for once, to be free from the guilt I have so long held inside me. Part of me regrets not dancing with Regina during the school dance. Then maybe I would have never come into contact with Keelan, and I wouldn't be in this position. But I am also glad to know that I didn't kill Keelan like everyone thought I did.

He lays a hand on my waist and takes my hand in his gracefully. Goosebumps travel up my side and to my neck. His dancing style is different from everyone else's. He's dancing like we're at a ball in the eighteen hundreds. I grab his stiff hand, but this time it doesn't bother me.

He twirls me and dips me to the ground. The top of his hair falls over his face, and his eyes peek between the strands. With him standing so close, his presence is almost unreal.

His eyes no longer looked like a predator, but now more like a human's. His eyes are the ones I once knew. It's a wonder how often his eyes change color. Originally, they are an emerald green, which I always thought was abnormal. But they change from black and green so often I can't tell how he's feeling at the moment.

"Are you ever going to tell me how old you are?" I ask.

I didn't know what I had expected him to say. He said he never witnessed the Salem witch trials. My mind wanders to the endless events in time. He could have lived through the American Revolution, or even the sinking of the Titanic. I imagine him fighting in a war with a musket in hand and charging into battle. No, that couldn't be Keelan. He is not the war type.

He smiles and ignores my question. I see in his eyes that he's enjoying himself. A light appears in his eyes that I haven't seen since we reconnected. His feet move in a way so gracefully. I don't understand what I am doing. My legs move underneath me without a thought of it. It's like I have danced like this for years now.

He pulls me tighter to his chest, the top of my head touches his chin. His pull becomes tighter, as if to never let me go. We sway against the beat of the music, following everyone else around us. Being with him felt right. I wish we could stay here forever.

"Are you ever going to talk to me, like really talk?" I ask.

The question catches him off guard. I don't think he expected me to be so blunt. As if someone is watching him, he looks at the dancing people.

"I haven't talked to you much because I am scared," we continue swaying in a circle. "I'm scared I might lose you." His voice shakes.

"I'm not going to die, Keelan."

"I don't think you know what you're getting yourself into. Samael, I mean Satan, doesn't care about human life. He will stop at nothing to find you."

"I—"

I can barely finish my sentence before his cold lips graze over mine

"I can't lose you, Juliet. You mean so much to me."

He crashes his lips into mine, and his frigid breath enters my mouth. I want to draw back in fear he may not be able to control himself, but his breath is steady, and he is still like a statue. His hands come further up my waist and he cups my face in his hands. I can't let go. His kiss is comforting. I try to unravel my feelings. Do I like him as a friend, or more?

My heart raced. My nerves are tingling from my head to my toes, even worse than where he was touching me. His lips are so smooth, with centuries' worth of blood dried into them. My body wants more, but I have to hold myself back and keep the lustful thoughts in my head.

He pulls back and rests his forehead on mine.

"I have wanted to do that for years now," he smiles.

The music stops and the crowd of people holler. Some continue to dance as if the music is still playing. Keelan eagerly looked to the stage. It's amazing how he can change his mind set so fast.

"Come on, we have to talk to Victoria."

He drags me along, maneuvering through the horde of drunks. He moves too fast and my legs can barely keep up.

"Hey, Victoria!" he calls.

As Victoria closes her laptop, she jumps, almost dropping her equipment on the floor.

"Keelan. Hey, how are you?" She puts her laptop in her bag, stuffing the chords into the side pockets.

"We need your help." He pulls me out from behind him.

Her eyes widen. She pauses.

"Is this the girl?" she whispers.

"Yes, this is Juliet. She needs your help."

I never thought of what I would say to her when I met her. She is much younger than I thought she would be. Her skin is perfect and glowing; she has no wrinkles and no strand of grey hair anywhere.

"I told Arthur I cannot become part of this."

"No, please. They won't tell me anything. I have to know—"

"Listen, I'm sure you are a nice girl, but I have things to do and places to be. I cannot interfere with vampire problems."

As she turns away, I grab her wrist. An electric charge surges through us, causing a spark between our skin. We both draw back at the same time. We hold our wrists in shock of what came between us. My hand tingles as if electrodes are placed on me, and powered by the lowest level.

"What was that?" I ask.

"I don't know," she glares. "I've touched other witches before, but the spark has never happened."

I can still feel the static from our touch. I had never been in the presence of another witch before, so I have nothing to compare it to. I'd believe it to be anything at this point.

My arm pulsates with pain. This time, the pain comes on suddenly without even a dull ache to warn me. My arm squeezes with a sharp pain, almost like a dagger being penetrated through it.

"Keelan. It hurts." I squeeze my hand to my stomach.

"Shit," Keelan glances at the dance floor. "They are here. The demons."

Large, hooded demons glide through the crowd unnoticed. The people continue to dance like nothing is going on. As the demons get closer, the pain gets worse. I sway side to side, Keelan keeping me balanced. It takes everything in me to hold down my vomit. It's making me weaker with every second.

"We have to go, now." Keelan takes my hand and pulls me to the exit.

"Wait," Victoria calls. "I'll help you. Follow me."

She grabs her laptop bag and pushes past us. The demons have noticed us now and are moving quicker. My nose fills with the smell of burning flesh and sulfur. The humming distracts me from walking, and I trip over my own feet.

Keelan lifts me up and throws me over his shoulder. Keelan follows Victoria out the back door, which was also used as an entrance. Party goers huddle around the door. Keelan pushes past them in a hurry. They are too inebriated to notice the fear in our eyes.

"Juliet, is that you?" a tiny voice calls. "Oh my god, what is going on. Keelan? Keelan, is that you?"

"Regina!"

Keelan ignores Regina's cries and follows Victoria to the van. Regina is running after us with tears streaming down her face.

"I have to talk to her." I try to kick my way off of Keelan's shoulder. "Please, let me go."

Tears block my vision as I struggle to get to her. The pain in my arm no longer exists, but the pain in my heart grows.

"Juliet, you can't. We have to go now." He throws me into the van and I crash against the side of it.

The van storms out of the parking lot and tosses me around. Keelan holds onto the handle above him and watches me on the ground. Tears roll down his face. I sob while the other two sit in silence.

"I wanted to see her," I sob.

"You know damn well I can't do that, Juliet," Keelan says.

As if ready to strike, his eyes grow black. The eyes of a monster stare down at me like this is my fault. I didn't know Regina would be at the club. I thought she would be home thinking I was dead. Now she knows I'm alive, and she won't hesitate to tell the entire school.

"She thought I was dead, because of you." I pound on his chest repeatedly. He doesn't move. He just takes the anger that I am giving him.

"She's my best friend."

CHAPTER EIGHT

From the cracks of the earth, guttural moans erupt. In their eternal terror, they scream for help. Their hands claw and grab for loose objects, or someone to pull through the cracks, so they too can suffer. Fires of orange and blue ascend with each wail. Their mouths breathe with smoke, and the skin around their faces are burnt to a crisp.

Sulfuric clouds turn red, and ashes fall from the clouds. The hurricane-like winds blow down trees and whisper through my hair. The strange but yet familiar feeling has me on edge..

"It was about time we met, Ms. Arden."

A low, deep voice echoes through the tree limbs. No one in any direction manifests themselves. Is it God speaking to me or something more sinister?

"Who are you?" I call.

A man in a dark suit comes forth from behind a winding tree. I can't see his face, but my heart pounds and my palms become sweaty. I look at my arm and the mark of the beast is bleeding. The bleeding won't stop, no matter how much I try to apply pressure.

"I remember you as a wee little baby." He makes a cradling motion.

"Are you the demon that gave me this?" I point to my arm, trying to catch the blood from dripping.

He laughs wickedly. He adjusts the watch on his wrist, as if he has somewhere to be.

"Call me Samael," he steps forward into the light of the moon. "You know, it has been extremely hard for my soldiers to find you. You are all over the place."

The cries of the lost souls screech louder in the distance as they sense their leader. He calls them his soldiers as if they are performing honorary duties. He had his demons come to my house and mark me, almost killing me in the process. Nothing about those creatures is heroic in the slightest.

"How do you know me?"

"Let's not worry about that now. We have business to discuss." He comes face to face with me. His devilish red eyes stare into my soul. "Now, wake up. Meet me in the place where your mother died."

My body's nerves shake as he disappears before my eyes. His body evaporates. A chorus of voices echoes in my head.

"Juliet, wake up. Wake up!"

My eyes flutter open. I lay, watching Keelan hover above me. His green eyes tremble and he grips onto my shoulders almost too tight. My heart begins to slow down back to it's normal rhythm.

"Are you okay?" He asks. "You were crying, in your sleep."

Victoria helps me from the bed and tips a cup of water to my lips. I slurp it down, water dripping down my neck.

"It was him," I gasp. "Samael."

"Does he know where you are? What does he want?" Keelan paces across the room.

"I don't think so. He said to meet him in the place where my mother died." Victoria and Keelan glance at each other.

Confused, I think of everything Edith had told me about her death. She told me she died just minutes after crashing into a semi truck. Ironically, I was born right as she entered the hospital. She hasn't even made it into a room yet and I came out in the gurney. She was in labor and didn't even know it. The blow to her head caused her to fall unconscious, so she didn't even know I was born.

That information isn't much to go on considering Edith has kept secrets from me all this time, and I believe this is one of those lies.

Victoria and Keelan look at me as if waiting for an answer. I sit with my feet over the bed nervously, thinking of what to say.

"I was told she died in a hospital. But I'm beginning to think that's a lie," I mutter. "it has to be someplace special if Samael wants me to meet him."

Victoria returns to the kitchen. Pots and pans clink against each other. Keelan stands in the corner of the room with his hand on his head. The tears in my eyes pool, but I suck them in, my lips quivering. I am tired of crying over everything. The guilt of not knowing eats at me.

"I have to know where she died. There has got to be a way."

"You're not seriously thinking of going to him, are you?" Keelan snaps.

"What other choice do I have? I won't be running the rest of my life from those demons."

Despite Keelan's efforts to be right, he's defeated. He slouches his shoulders. I can't run from the demons forever. I can stay in one place for a short amount of time before the demons rush in and take me. That is not a life worth living.

Victoria comes out of the kitchen with a steaming mug in hand. I pull the blanket over me, preparing for what she has to say.

"I have an idea."

"I am down for anything," I suggest.

"I can project your soul to hell," She says.

"Anything except that."

The thought of going to hell frightens me. I may have already seen it in my dreams. If it was as bad as my Edith says it is, why would I go down there willingly? Hell is where Samael wants me to be. Why would I give him the satisfaction of entering his territory?

"No. Are you mad?" Keelan coughs.

"I have done it before. I performed the spell on a woman who wanted to confront her adulterous husband. I have the power to do it." Victoria hands me the mug. "You have to figure out where your mother died. Why not ask her yourself?"

The minute the steam enters my nose it calms me. Talking to my mother is something I never thought I'd be able to do in my lifetime, or at all. I never thought much of talking with the dead. I never learned how to do it properly. I am not educated enough to do so. I'm not even sure I want to learn how. Using a ouija board is nothing compared to actually going to hell. This is next level witchcraft.

"Why do you think she is in hell? All witches roam the earth when they die."

Victoria glances at Keelan, and me with her eyebrows creased.

"I thought you knew."

Keelan's eyes turn black.

"Your mother tried to sacrifice you to Samael. Anyone who knows about summoning knows that if you summon the devil, your soul belongs to him"

My heart drops. The dream, it all makes sense now. The woman is my mother, and the baby wass me. I was the helpless baby who cried for her mother. I'm uncertain if I should feel rage or grief. How could my mother, whom I share a gift with, sacrifice me to someone so vile and evil?

"Why would you say that?" Keelan pins Victoria against the wall.

A painting shatters to the floor, causing Victoria to bleed from her head. She raises her hand and pushes Keelan to the adjacent wall without touching him. He crashes into the wall, leaving a broken pot of plants scattered on the floor.

"I thought she knew," Victoria stands face to face with Keelan. "How was I supposed to know she didn't know a thing about her mother?"

The pressure of guilt sweeps over me like a wave. I'm oblivious to anything about my mother's history. Now I understand why Edith kept everything from me regarding my mother. She too was ashamed of her, and I didn't blame her, not even an ounce. Edith was trying to protect me the entire time. She was trying to save my soul every time she took me to church or prayed over me. I took advantage of that. How can I face her now after all that has come to face?

I have no other way to talk to my mother. She might even tell me why she tried to sacrifice me to Samael. Deep inside my mind, I feel she only did it for selfish reasons, but any reason at all would cause me to hold a grudge. How could she call herself a mother for what she did to me? I was a small and defenseless little baby, and she had the audacity to give my life away. *Mother of the year.*

"I want to talk to my mom."

"Are you sure? Can we find another way?" Keelan proposes.

"No. I have to do this. Not only to sort out this mess, but to find out why she sold my soul when it was not hers to give."

Victoria takes us to a hatch that leads to the basement. It's musty, and spiders crawl along the walls. Even dead cockroaches lay on their backs. She must have not used it often due to its lack of cleanliness. The wooden stairs wobble with each step descending into the dark.

A dimly lit lightbulb hangs in the middle of the room, swinging by a small wire. The air is thick, making me short of breath, or maybe it's the nerves compressing my lungs. I'm going to meet my mother for the first time in eighteen years. I should be happy for this opportunity, but something gives me the opposite feeling.

Victoria sweeps the floor before us, and a carving of a pentagram emerges from the dirt. The candles ignite around us, without a flame from a match. I stand at the top of the pentagram, and from my studies of the pentacle, I'm at the spirit point of the star. I know this is where I have to be.

Victoria fumbles through a thick book. I wait patiently for her instructions. My palms become sweaty and my head is dazy. Keelan comes to me and stands at my shoulder.

"Are you sure about this?" He breaths. "You can back out."

"This has to be done," I nod.

Victoria directs me to the middle of the pentacle. My arm pulses with pain, but I stay calm through it. Victoria puts a candle on each point of the star and ignites it with her magic.

"Keelan, go in the circle with her."

"Why?"

"You need to make sure she is breathing."

Keelan steps one foot inside the pentacle. "Are you telling me she could die doing this?"

Victoria flips through more pages. "It's a possibility, but highly unlikely."

Victoria's monotone voice creates a tension in my lungs. I know I'll come out of this alive.

Keelan kneels beside me with his eyes fixed on every move I make. His lower lip trembles.

"I don't know if I should say goodbye or see you later." he chuckles.

I lift my body to him and kiss him. I pull away, but he stays connected to my lips, following me back down to the ground.

"Let your mind take you where you need to go."

She begins to chant a spell in a language I'm not all too familiar with. Most of it sounds Latin, but that's normal with most spells.

"*Demons of the lake of fire,*" The temperature changes as she speaks. "*Release this girl of her physical chains. Let the spirits guide her to the underworld.*"

Keelan squeezes my hands. The blood rushes from my feet to my burnt arm. I can't distract myself from the pain anymore. I'm sure my arm is bleeding. Everything is warm. I can't hear Victoria speak. Keelan looks down at me with worry in his eyes. He screams something I can't hear. His hands are soiled in my blood.

He keeps holding his hands out in front of him, turning to Victoria with fear in his eyes.

The picture of Keelan fades to black. Nothing surrounds me but the clothes on my back. I feel no wind, no temperature, not even the Earth below my feet. The ground is hard, that much I know. I can't see what material I'm walking on.

I walk further into the dark. The loneliness haunts me. I hear a high-pitched noise in the distance, still no sight of anything. I walk faster, my feet taking over despite my fear of the unknown.

A bright light shines feet away from me. As I walk further, the light is split into two torches encased in blue fire. I go to the torches and find a complete drop off from the ground. I look into the abyss; it leads to the lake of fire. Screams of the tortured fill my ears, the sudden screeching pierces my ears. The souls of the lake reach at my feet, trying to pull me in with them.

"Hey, who are you?"

I jump, and a hooded figure stands behind me. This time the robe is red, not black, like the demons who came after me. The figure is way taller than the demons, and he holds a spear in his gloved hand.

"Who are you?" I reply.

He pushes his hood over his head. I expected a creature so ugly would be underneath it, but I had never seen something so normal in my life. It's almost hysterical. His clean-shaven face looks just as confused as I am.

"I am the gatekeeper of souls." He stands on the edge of the cliff. "They call me Leviathan."

I chuckle to myself. He isn't so scary as people make him out to be. He appears as a normal human, with brown hair and dull grey eyes. In demonology, he's depicted as a giant serpent like sea creature. And I thought I had to battle a dangerous monster.

"You're not dead. I get a lot of you living people down here." He rests his spear on the torch. "Did a spell go wrong? I can help you get out."

"Aren't you supposed to be guarding the gate?" I ask.

"Being funny, aren't we? If you must know, I was otherwise engaged with Asmodeus. Cranky little bitch he is. He is always going after the young and beautiful," He laughs.

I gaze down to the screaming souls, wondering how I'd ever get to my mother or if he would even let me. He seems more like a jokester than a demon and gatekeeper. Such a child.

"So this is hell? Doesn't seem so scary as everyone makes it out to be."

He laughs, stirring his spear into the lake of fire.

"Oh, this isn't all of it. Go down a few more levels and they've got the most ruthless murderers hanging from their eye sockets."

I didn't need intense and gruesome imagery. I'd rather stay right where I am and find my mom. I hope she was at least on this level so I wasn't going on a quest to find her.

"I came to see my mother."

"Ahh, missing your mother, huh?" He cracks his knuckles

"Not exactly. I need to get information from her. She kind of sold my soul." I hesitate.

His eyes widen. I'm not sure If I should have kept that last part to myself or not. I don't want him and the other demons after me in my spirit body or have a free for all with my physical body. My spiritless body pretty much gives them free rein to do as they please with my body.

"Oh, mother of the year. Who are you looking for?" He asks.

"Esther Arden."

"You're joking, right?" He barks.

I shake my head. He laughs, but his voice turns to a low, demonic growl.

"You're the girl that Samael has been after."

"What's new? Can I talk to my mother or not?"

He crosses his arms and picks up his spear, caressing the fine points on the spear. I fear he might try to keep me here, only to gain the glory of it when Samael finds out the gatekeeper of souls caught the witch.

"Yeah, I guess I can let you through but on only one condition," He said. "Tell Samael he needs to fight his own fight."

I wasn't sure what to do with that information, whether he meant it figuratively or he was being serious. I would not stay here any longer than I had to. I couldn't risk being seen by too many demons. Word would get out and Samael would trap me here for eternity. Leviathan seemed like he didn't really follow the rules.

Leviathan points his spear over the fiery lake. A gondola appears out of a cloud of mist. The boat looks small enough to fit two bodies, him and the souls he'd take to their eternity of torture.

"This will take you where you need to go." I step into the gondola and he pushes it away with his foot.

Before my eyes, his face transforms into a reptilian creature and grows hundreds of feet above me. His serpent body looks down at me.

"Oh by the way, don't let the souls touch you." His long serpent body disappears into the lake of fire.

I compress my body, so I'm as far away from the edges as possible. I can't imagine what it would be like to be pulled into the lake, even as a spirit. Would my body wake? Or would I become a tortured soul of the underworld?

It seems as if I had sailed this lake for ages. I can see how one would lose track of time here; there is no time. I wonder how long I've actually been in the spirit state. It could be minutes or even hours. I can't help but think of what Keelan is doing right now, even Regina and my Aunt Edith. I miss them all, and it tore my heart to pieces not knowing if they are okay or where they are at.

The boat stops at a wooden dock. It must have been hiding in the mist, because I hadn't seen it before. On the dock, a wooden sign reads the name: Esther Arden. In plain sight, she is right ahead of me. I want to turn away, but I wouldn't be here in the first place without her.

I walk further to find a cave with bars towering from top to bottom, screwed into the rock on each end. The bars are rusted and dead vines wrap around them. I don't understand the decorations, but everything is dead, just like the souls it captured.

"Hello?"

Chains rattle against the rocks. It's too dark for me to see what was lurking in there. This is it. I am finally meeting my mother. I wonder if she would be anything like my Aunt Edith. Most kids dreamt of talking to a lost parent. I'm not one of them. In fact, I feel the complete opposite. I don't want to do this. I don't know her. I already hate her. I don't even want any type of relationship with her.

"Esther?"

"Who is asking? Mammon?" The voice echoes.

She comes into the light of the fire. Her grey hair is ratted over her face. The chains bind her feet and hands, but give her enough room to maneuver the cave. Her bare feet are singed from the coal, and pus filled boils line her legs and arms. She smells of rotten eggs and guilt.

"Who are you? What do you want? Are you here to take me to Asmodeus?"

"No."

She walks back into the cave. Already done with me and she hasn't even looked me in the eye.

"I'm the baby you sacrificed eighteen years ago." I don't hesitate to let her know who I am.

She stops. Her head turns, and she eyes me in her peripheral vision. Walking back to the bars, she moves the hair from her face.

"Juliet? Is that you? I can't believe you are here." She reaches out to me behind the bars. She grabs hold of me by the collar of my shirt.

I pry her hands off me.

"I am only here for one thing. This is not a reunion, Esther."

She shutters at the mention of her real name, and not by the nickname she expects me to give her. *Mother.*

"You've made it clear you were never truly my mother. Edith is a better mother than you could ever be. I thought she hated me, but she was only trying to protect me from the mess you pulled me into."

She sobs, and then suddenly she turns quiet. Her face turns deadpan. It's like she had never cried. I have no empathy for her. I should be the one crying. But it would only make me look weak. She is the weak one. How could she expect me to call her mother after all the shit she did to me?

"I need to know where you died." I kneel on the ground in front of her. "I have to meet Samael for some business."

She shakes her head, almost like she's having a seizure. Drool emerges from the corner of her mouth. She holds her head as if to stop the shaking. Her eyes move in a manner that's haunting. The whites of her eyes show through and then return to their color.

"Stull," she says. "Stull, Kansas is where I died. The cemetery on the hill."

What an unusual place to be. Stull is hundreds of miles away from home. I don't want to go into details of what got her there. I stand and brush myself off. I have heard all I need to knowI don't want to make small talk, but something inside my gut tells me I shouldn't leave yet. Out of nowhere, a thought inside of me clicked. I have to know.

"Why did you do it? What was so important that you thought sacrificing your innocent baby would be worth it?"

I'm not sure if I want to know the answer to that, but the words spill out of my mouth without warning. I know that if I don't ask this now, I may never be able to again. After this, I want nothing to do with her. I will fight hard to make sure she isnt even in my memory anymore.

"I was trying to resurrect your father."

All this time I believed my mother was someone to look up to. I wanted to be a powerful witch just like her. Everyday I imagined how my life would be if she was there to raise me, and not my Aunt. All of those thoughts shatter to pieces in one sentence.

I never knew my father, or really anything about him. Aunt Edith would never talk about him. Whenever I mentioned him, she would always redirect the subject. After asking for so many years, I eventually quit. But during all those years, I made up false memories of what he would have been like. Would he have the same hair and eyes as me or look the complete opposite? It's possible I inherited some of his features. He could be tall or short, although I'm pretty sure I'm not going to get any taller than this. For a while I thought maybe he was still out there, living his life without a care for me. Maybe he was looking for me somehow. But this entire time he's been dead.

"He's dead?" I turn away from her. "Why didn't he come back? I assume the sacrifice didn't work since I'm still alive."

She shakes her head. "He is still dead, and Satan still owns your soul."

I don't know a thing about sacrificial rituals, let alone necromancy. It's not something I have an interest in learning or even knowing anything about. Nothing makes sense. If the sacrifice didn't work, then how is my father still dead? If it would have worked, I'd be dead and Esther would be living her life with her lover. How could my father even be okay with her actions? I am his daughter, too. She is beyond selfish.

"What's his name?" My lips quiver.

"Michael Arden."

I gasp at the sound of his name. Even with both parents dead, I have his last name. I thought maybe my mother had given me her maiden name. Edith still uses her late husband's last name. So I know the two aren't the same. In spite of her death, I still wonder how she gave me his last name.

"Well, thanks for the disappointment, Esther. I must be off. Important things to do."

I go to the gondola. I hear her screams and cries from behind me. Part of me wants to turn back and look her in the face, but she isn't worth it. Nothing she ever did was worth it. I hate her, and that is something I will never regret.

"Juliet, wait."

I hesitate to face her, but this may be the last time I ever see her. I want to fully see her for who she is. A monster.

"Your father was an amazing man. He was gifted, just like you."

"Reditus."

***

I gasp, and the cold air enters my lungs. I cough so much I vomit. My heart is racing too fast. I feel I may faint. The light above me shines too bright for my eyes. I must have been in the dark for too long.

"Juliet, are you okay?" Keelan grabs me by the shoulders. "What happened?"

He pushes my hair out of my face. Sweat forms in all places of my body. I still can't see very well. Everything is a blur. I can feel the temperature again, and the touch of Keelan. I am back to my own reality.

"How long was I gone?" I pant.

"Almost three hours." Keelan squeezes my hand to his chest. "I thought you were slipping. Your heart was barely beating."

He pulls me to him, face buried in his cold chest. I listen, but there is no pounding of the heart. Everything is completely still. The void in his chest is soothing.

I struggle to my feet. The pentacle becomes a haze in the dirt. I hold on to Keelan as he leads me up the stairs. Victoria follows behind us with the grimoire in her hand; she is silent. Part of me feels like she knew the conversation I had between Esther and I.

I'm not prepared for Keelan's bombarding of questions. He's patient with me as he sits next to me, hands over mine, and I sip on my tea. I can't think of what to say to them first. What hell really looks like, what my mother looked like, who I met along the way. It's all so flustering.

I can't tell Keelan where Esther died. He will stop at nothing to keep me from going. I don't even know how I would get there. Kansas is over a thousand miles away from here. Keelan won't take me, and I'm not sure Victoria would be down for the ride either.

"Is everything okay?" Keelan asks.

"She died in Stull, Kansas," I gulp my tea down. "And before you ask me, Esther is a monster. She is not my mother, she never will be.

Keelan lowers his eyes. I don't want him feeling bad for me or anyone. I will never regret the remorse I have for Esther. I will always live with the last memory of her in hell. Chains will forever bind her. There will be no returning to hell in a later time and asking her to be in my life. It will never willingly go back there. If I'm ever so unfortunate to spend an eternity in hell, I want her to watch what she did to me.

"I have to go. This has to end."

CHAPTER NINE

October 2016

"Ignite. Dammit, candle, make a flame!"

"Are you sure you are saying it right?" Keelan asked.

"Yes, I am sure. Now, quiet, unless you know Latin."

The flame ignited the smallest flame. I want to give up, I can't do it. The instructions make it easier said than done. If I can't do a simple candle lighting spell, how can I ever prove myself a powerful witch like my mother?

Keelan read through more of the grimoires from many years back. His eyes moved steadily through each page. He read better than I, so I trusted he would make a thorough reading. He was much better at following directions.

"Articulate the words."

"I'm not fluent in Latin, Keelan. I am trying." I pouted.

I look at the pentacle to my right, absorbing the energy it leaked. I hoped doing this would gain enough power to light this candle. Even the moon was at its peak and I still can not do this simple task.

I wished more than anything I'd turn into the great witch my mother was. I know little about her, only that she was an extraordinary at the craft. My Aunt Edith does not talk a lot about her sister, so I know nothing of how my mother really was.

"I can't do it." I cried.

"Yes you can, just breathe."

"No, this will never work."

I feel myself losing the charge from the moon. It's slipping away from me, and regret courses over me. I am such a disappointment to all of witch kind.

"Maybe, you need to take a break."

Keelan came to me and gently closed the book, eyes on me the entire time. He only did that when he was trying to gain someone's attention. He was so patient with me, and with everyone he knew. I couldn't have asked for a more caring friend other than Regina.

I balled my fists. I was too angry to give up now. I have to get this. I will get this.

"Ignite," the candle sparked. "Ignite"

The sparks stopped, and I threw the books across the room. They scatter all around us. I let out a scream. I cannot hold this frustration in any more.

"Juliet, stop," Keelan rushed to the floor to pick up the books. "Stop it. Look what you are doing."

The books went up in flames. It spread like a wildfire. The fire destroyed everything it touched. The books and the papers, to the pillows and blankets. The room was going up in flames. I fall to the ground and rummage through the untouched books. I search for any useful spell to stop the fire. I can't find anything as the fire grows.

"Juliet, what are you doing?" He coughs.

"I can fix this."

It becomes harder to breathe as the smoke thickens the air. My lungs burn with every inhale. The fire tears through the wallpaper beside me.

"Come on, we have to get out of here."

Keelan lunges to me, and a wall of fire separates us. The fire comes over my face. My face was engulfed with fire. I fall to the ground and try to put out the fire. It burns more than anything I have ever experienced. I am in shock. I don't know what to do.

"Keelan," I cried.

I looked over the wall of fire. I held my face and realized I was bleeding. I catch a glimpse of Keelan's feet on the ground. He wasn't moving.

"Keelan, wake up!"

I search for anything to put out the fire. There was nothing to help me get over the wall of fire. Keelan lay helpless, and I could not get to him.

The window bursted, and glass flew in the air.. I shielded my face from the sparkling debris. Maybe this was a sign. It was a way out, but I can't leave Keelan. He will surely die.

"Wake up!"

He's dead. He's dead. He's dead. There was no way to wake him, and his body would be too heavy to pull through the window. He was dead, and it was all my fault.

I crawl out the window and fall off the roof. Landing on the ground, I notice a swarm of fire trucks come speeding in the neighborhood. The bright lights lit up the entire block. Next, an emergency vehicle parks on the side of the road and two people come rushing from out of it.

"Ma'am, was there anyone else in there?"

I nodded, and they ran into the house.

The EMTs tend to my face. I don't pay attention to what they do. I felt no pain, and that may be from the adrenaline and shock. It seemed like the firefighters had been in there for an eternity. They had to find Keelan, they just had to.

The firefighters came running out. Keelan's limp body was flopping around in their arms. He was completely lifeless. I pushed away the EMTs as they grabbed for me. I ran to the firefighters.

"Is he alive? Keelan. Wake up," The EMTs came to my side and grabbed me. "Keelan. No."

They rested his lifeless body on a gurney and on the emergency vehicle. He was dead, and it was all because of me.

"Where are we?"

Drool runs down the side of my mouth. I look outside the window and see nothing but miles of farmland surrounding us. The green rolling hills repeat in a pattern, and the barrels of hay are neatly spread out. Cows graze in the pastures, with their calves nursing on them.

I have never seen something so beautiful. The open road and beautiful landscape is a refreshing scene. People always make Kansas out to be such a boring state, but how can that be when I could look at this horizon for hours?

"Just now entering Kansas," Keelan sighs.

The carpet of the van smells of must and earth. Victoria must have not thought to clean the van, since it may not have been cleaned since it was made. A lot of the parts look original as manufactured. Although outdated, it still has a lot of style and personality.

Keelan holds a large map. He looks perplexed, assuming the lines and numbers confuse him. He was never comfortable using electronics, so he wanted to go old school and navigate by paper.

"Stull is so tiny," He says, squinting on the page. "Why would he be here?"

"There is an old legend that involves the cemetery. Something about it being a gate to hell," Victoria adds.

"Wow, I guess that explains why he hasn't appeared anywhere but your dreams. He can only travel through certain portals."

Samael is limited in his ability to transport, so he lets his demons do his dirty work. He must not have been that powerful as people make him out to be. Hopefully meeting with him will give me an idea of what he wants and what his weaknesses are. I don't expect to kill him. How could I anyway? I need to make him weak. Whatever his plans are, they are up to no good.

I notice Victoria's purse below her. A wallet and phone peak out of the top.I have to call Edith. I have to apologize to her for how badly I have treated her all these years. I know the truth now, and all I want is to make peace with her. I have to do this, because if I die, she will never know.

"Victoria, can I borrow your phone?"

Keelan slams the map down, crinkling the edges. He twists his head and glares at me.

"You can't do that."

"I have to apologize to my aunt. For everything I did to her."

Without looking at Keelan, Victoria reaches in her purse and hands me her phone. I wasn't sure if she heard who I was calling, but I won't take any chances of passing this up. Keelan returns to the map angrily.

"Hello."

"Aunt Edith, it's me, Juliet," My hands shake. I can hear her breathing. "I just want to let you know I am okay, and I am sorry."

"Oh, Juliet. Where are you? Why are you sorry?"

"I am doing something important," Keelan eyes me in the mirror. "I wanted to tell you I am sorry for treating you terribly. You never deserved it. I now know why you are so protective."

Silence rings through the phone. I want to hang up. I don't want to hear what she has to say. What if she doesn't accept my apology? If I got out of this alive, I would have no one to go back to.

"So it took you this long to figure it out, huh? I never wanted this fate for you," she breathes. "I knew what was to happen on your birthday, and I am sorry for not being there to protect you."

I smile. Tears consume my eyes. I want to go to her and hug her. I miss her. I always thought she was the evil one, and now I know who the evil one truly was.

"Whatever you are doing, I trust you will do the right thing." The line goes dead.

I feel a release, a tension that I never realized was there until this very moment.. Years of hurt and anger lift off my shoulders, all because of one phone call and a visit to my mother in hell. She trusted I would do the right thing, but I'm not sure if what I am doing is the right thing. I was going to make a deal with the devil myself.

***

The cemetery is small, and easily hidden from the outside world. A strange energy radiates off it like it's a radioactive factory. As we walk further into the cemetery, the temperature drops so low I think we'll freeze to death. The gravestones lay crooked and chipped. The dead grass crunches beneath our feet. Everything is dead here. This has to be the place.

"What a janky cemetery," Keelan states.

The sun is setting, and the cemetery becomes a haven for the dead. The dark that surrounds us creeps at every corner. We come to a slab of stone that is a few feet wide. No walls surround it, but clearly a building once stood here, possibly a church. It's too cliché. The gate to hell is an old church.

"Do you feel that?" Victoria stops.

"Feel what?" Keelan asks.

The vibrations surrounding us increase. Victoria and I both feel the negative energy surrounding the old church. My heart pounds, and I can tell Victoria's is too. We call it witch intuition. We can sense all energies, negative or positive. I hadn't practiced magic much for the past few months, but I know what it's supposed to feel like.

"Are we early?" Keelan laughs.

There is no one around. No demons, and certainly no king of hell. Surely he must have known I'd be here. I saw him in my dream. This is where he wants me to meet him. I'm getting more anxious by the second.

An old farmhouse rests on the border of the cemetery. No lights came from inside and one old truck was parked in the driveway. I wonder how many people are driven off this property from the homeowners. Teenagers would come out here to investigate the supernatural, and would be driven out by fear or the people next door.

I search each corner of the old church, looking for a clue to what I must do. Upon looking, I find droplets of dried blood. The cold stone is covered in blood all around it. Engraved on the top of the rock is a sigil, the sigil of Baphomet. It's like the one burnt into my hand.

My arm sears with pain as I edge closer to the stone. I know what I have to do in order to call Samael forth.

"What are you doing?" Keelan grabs my hand. "If you die, your soul will go to hell."

"He already owns my soul."

I rest my hand on the rigged stone. My hand burns and I swear I can hear sizzling from beneath. The pain isn't enough for me to cry, but it is like tiny needles pricking my skin. The blood oozes from my hand, consuming the stone in crimson.

The wind stirs through our hair, and the leaves fly around us. The stone cracks, and the smell of sulfur rises out of it. Victoria runs to the newest tree to hide, all while holding her books in hand. Keelan remains next to me, holding my hand.

Flashes of light beam around us, each revealing naked demons. They aren't wearing robes like last time. Each move causes their scaly, dry flesh to crack. Their legs are not of a human but of a creature I have never seen in my life. Their eyes are filled with a blackness that makes me uneasy. Horns grow out of their skulls, so sharp it could cut glass. These are the demons I have been waiting to meet. They are the demons from my nightmares.

The crack in the ground roars like thunder and fire rises above us. Keelan squeezes my hand tighter than before. Whether he is scared or just trying to protect me, I don't know.

Smoke slithers along our feet, and the tall man from my dreams stands before us. He looks nothing like he had appeared in my dreams. Devil horns poke through his head, and blood drips around the seam. His gigantic wings follow behind him, as if to shield other's from prying ears. His red eyes glow. I can't look at him for more than a few seconds. He's come here to do business, and if he's going to get what he wants, he's going to scare me into it.

"Finally, we meet in person," he smiles. "The pleasure is all mine." He holds out his hand and bows. I look at him and I refuse to touch his filthy hands.

Keelan pulls me closer to him. We now stand shoulder to shoulder. I'm too frightened to move. I want to tell him this wasn't the time to play hero; this is my fight. I never could have imagined I'd be in the presence of the almighty evil of the world. If only my aunt could see me now. She would be on her knees, praying to God.

"Wise of you to meet me, Juliet. Very wise." Samael glances at Keelan. "And who is this lovely gentleman?"

"What do you want?" I ask.

I scoff at his need to have a normal conversation. I didn't come here to make friends with him. Whatever he wants, I refuse to do. I'll be kind enough to listen to him. But I don't see any of this going well. I prepare myself for anything he'd say. Because he is the Lord of darkness and all things evil, I expect him to order me to do his bidding, to kill for him.

"We can't have any distractions." He waves his hand, and Keelan goes flying, hitting a tree.

My legs itch to run to Keelan, but I fear my fate would be worse than his. Keelan's limp body lay underneath the tree Victoria is hiding behind. She creeps around the trunk, peeking at Keelan, trying not to be seen by Samael.

"I see you have brought another witch with you. How fascinating. We don't need her either." He waves his hand as before. Victoria drops her books to the ground and falls next to Keelan.

My heart is racing now. I brought them for a reason, and now they lay unconscious under a tree. I'm alone and powerless. I can't stand against Samael and his demons by myself. Samael wants me alone, and that is what he will get.

"Fantastic. Now, let's get down to business." He circles around me. His evil eyes pierce into my soul; the soul that had always been his. His shoulder touches mine as he circles around me. His yellow claws scraped across my face.

"Perfect," He mumbles.

"Don't get any ideas."

He laughs, "Oh dear child, I wouldn't take another man's woman. How ill do you think of me?"

I stand still as ever. I wait for him to say something. The wait feels like an eternity.

The demons surrounding us perch like statues, completely still. Their faces are still covered. Their presence, though, sends a tingling sensation down my spine. If Samael wasn't here to control them they'd lunge after me and tear me to pieces.

"Your magic is powerful. I've known it for almost one hundred years now." He gestures.

"What do you mean, one hundred years?" I ask.

"Has no one told you?" He smiles. "Your birth was prophesied by those who practiced divination. I couldn't let that power go to waist. So I waited till you were born, and then another eighteen years to finally get ahold of you"

Most of what he says is complete bullshit, but even Keelan had to have known about the future. He said he was chosen to protect me, and they trained him for this particular task. He had to protect me from ever being near Samael and discovering his sinister plans.

Keelan knew what was to come, and he tried everything to keep me from furthering my knowledge. Only his passion for me got in the way. Why couldn't they have trained me to fight him, instead of being the helpless little girl I have been this entire time.

"I need you to summon a powerful demon. The most powerful witch ever to live."

How can he be serious? A summoning spell that almost any witch could do. How low could he possibly go to ask for help from a regular witch? He waited one hundred years for a simple witch to perform a spell? He must not have been so desperate since he waited for so long. Or, he's trying to keep the blood off his hands.

"Why do you need my help? You're the ruler of hell. I'm sure you could handle it on your own."

He lunges at me with his burning hands around my throat. His eyes are red like the fire that consumes him. He is so close I can almost see into his soul, if he even has one.

"Do not disrespect me, or you will end up in the same place as your filthy mother. Do not question me. I know who made you," He growls.

He lets go of my throat, and the air returns to my lungs with a sting. His print leaves burns etched into my throat. It tingles so much it feels like it is boiling my skin.

"I cannot summon this being, because an angel banished her. She roams freely in the depths of hell. She cannot return to the actual world, this disgusting pit you call Earth."

A demon that is banished by an angelic can't travel through worlds freely, and only an angelic can release them from their banishment. The thing about the angelics is that they can banish them, but none of them dare to release them back into the world. That is what makes their magic absolute.

"Sorry to disappoint you. I am just a regular witch. You have been wasting your time searching for the wrong witch," I sneer.

"No, dear, you are the right witch for the job. You must not know about your family lineage," he laughs."

His voice turns into a deep rattle, something like a snake.

"Dear child, did your mother not tell you anything about your father while on your brief trip to hell? So sorry about that reunion by the way, such a shame."

Esther held back from telling me anything about my father. Maybe this was the reason she didn't tell me about him. Samael needs an angelic to do the job. If my mother was a witch, then my father must have been an angel. I have the power to summon and banish. This is a gift I ever wanted to bear.

It's unheard of for a witch and an angel to mate. For witches, it won't matter, but for angels, it goes against their entire being. I don't know how they got around it. Someone must have tried to break them apart. I can't even understand how they were able to have me.

"My father is an angel? That would make me?"

"Half angel, half witch. Perfect for the job," He says.

A tear trickles down my face. I can't handle the amount of secrets that have been unraveling the past few days. Nobody should have to go through this, not magical or non-magical. *I am an abomination.*

"Did I pluck a heart string? How touching."

"What do you need me to do?" I ask, annoyed.

His evil grin widens. The white of his teeth glow in the moonlight. His sinister brain was clicking and thinking of ways to torment me more. It brings him pleasure to see the demise of others.

"You are going to summon my lover, Lilith."

CHAPTER TEN

"Wake up. Juliet, please."

I'm shaken from my deep sleep. Keelan kneels above me, shaking my shoulders. I can barely see any light. Only four small torches are lit around us.

"Where are we?" I sit up.

Keelan pats my back and keeps me steady. I rub my eyes, trying to gain my vision back.

"I don't know what happened." I struggle to stand. "Last I remember, we were in the cemetery, and you were unconscious"

I look at Keelan. His forehead streams blood. This isn't a good sign. He should have healed by now. I no longer feel the energy like I did at the cemetery. It is a void of nothingness. It's like I've been cut off from all magic. I am numb and I feel so alone.

"Keelan, your head is bleeding."

He touches his head and notices his fingers are covered in blood.

"You are too." I look at my hand. The mark is bleeding, and it appears to be freshly cut. I'm surprised my hand hasn't fallen off from an infection. I observe where I'm laying. A puddle of blood surrounds Keelan and me, and it seeps into my clothes. Our blood mixes together.

I peer at Keelan. His eyes fade to black. He is no longer himself, but consumed by the monster that controls him.

"Juliet, please stand back," he backs up to the wall. "I can't be near you. I don't know what is going on. I can usually control my impulses."

I stand in the middle of the room. Victoria is nowhere to be found. She wouldn't be helpful, though. If Keelan is bleeding, then our magic must not work either. This is a trap. Keelan is the killer, and I am the victim.

A metal hatch creaks above us and a small light shines through. The room is ignited enough for us to see how big the place is. The high ceiling and sanded stones make it impossible to scale. There is no way out of this hole.

"Finally, you are awake," a voice echoes. "I want to have a little fun before we get down to business."

Samael calls from above, his demonic voice echoes off the walls.

"There is no magic in here, but there is one wooden stake."

Keelan's breathing becomes heavy. His fingers twitch beside him. I notice he is losing control. I have to find a way to defend myself. I have to find a way out of here before he kills me.

"Keelan's predator instincts are consuming him, Juliet. I suggest you fix the problem," He laughs.

Keelan's black eyes glimmer at me with rage. The blood is now dripping from my hand, so much so I can hear the drops hitting the ground. There is no place for me to hide. I focus on the wooden stake that is on the floor. I can't kill him. I refuse to.

Keelan lunges at me with his fangs out. I dodge to the floor, banging my head against the cold stone. It disorients me for a quick moment. As I regain my vision, I see Keelan crawling to grab my feet.

"Keelan, stop. Listen to me." I kick his face, but he is unfazed. "You can control it. You have to."

"I can't help myself, Juliet, "He claws at my foot as I reach for the stake. I can't resist you."

My body scrapes against the rocks. I feel his claws against my ankles. He twisted me over onto my back. The light was still shining through the skylight above. Keelan's contorts over my body, each of his limbs holding mine down. My strength is no match for his. He is crushing my body with every move.

I come face to face with him. The veins in his face swell with rage. His teeth are sharp like a knife. This is the true Keelan, the one I wish I'd never see in my lifetime. I'm going to die. My lover is going to kill me. No fiber in my body or magic spell can help me now.

I hold on to hope as my fingertips brush the wooden stake. Almost there. Keelan's claws dug into my skin. He takes hold of my free hand and sniffs it like a wild animal. He licks his lips and bites into my hand. I'm sure the teeth went all the way through.

The pain is nothing like I have felt before. It's more painful than when I had the mark burned into my hand. What makes it worse is looking into his eyes and seeing the killer he is made to be, the killer I can't deny I am falling in love with. He is slowly killing me and he doesn't even realize it.

"Stop, please," I scream. My body is in too much shock to make me cry.

Blood streams down his mouth and neck. My arm becomes a red and mutilated mess. His teeth sink into my skin and all down my arm. The sound of his fangs piercing my skin is maddening. With each bite, I feel myself losing my grip on reality. The adrenaline pushes the pain away. I'm slowly drifting to the point I cannot hear anything but the beat of my heart and the distant sound of the afterlife.

"Okay, that was fun," Samel laughs from above.

Keelan's grip on my body loosens, and his eyes return to its original green color. His eyes explore me in confusion. He shakes as he sees the blood that covers his arms. He touches the trail of blood that covers his face.

"What, what happened?" He shakes his head. "Juliet, why was your arm-?"

I lay on the ground. His voice is muffled. He realizes his teeth prints are on my arms. My blood runs through the cracks of the stone. He tastes my blood encased in his teeth and lips. If he tastes anymore of my blood, it may send him into another frenzy, and I don't have the energy to protect myself again.

"No. I didn't," He lifts his body from me. "This isn't real. I almost killed you."

He backs away from me with his back against the wall. Tears fill his evergreen eyes. I want to be mad at him, but I know he was under another's control. This is all Samael's fault. This is all a game to him.

"Juliet, I am so sorry," He cries.

I race to him, but he stops me.

"This wasn't your fault. He made you lose control." I sway back and forth. The amount of blood I'm losing will soon send me into shock and probably kill me. I kneel in front of him.

"Juliet, stay with me," He cradles me in his arms. "Stay with me." He slaps my face, attempting to bring me back.

A boulder in front of us opens. Two robed demons approach us. One pushes Keelan away from me. The other pours a liquid into my mouth. It is almost tasteless, but has a hint of battery acid. I choke on the substance. It burns my throat and sizzles the membranes.

"No, what are you doing?" Keelan screams.

I regain my full consciousness. My vision is no longer blurry. Keelan sits in the fetal position with his head buried in his legs. His sobs are powerful. I want him. I want him to hold me and tell me everything is going to be alright. This is terrifying for the both of us.

The demons lift me from the ground. Their massive hands curl under my shoulders. I wince, but I don't feel any more pain. My arm, still bloodied, isn't actively bleeding, but healing itself. The concoction they gave me must have had healing properties.

"No, where are you taking her," Keelan calls out.

The demons pull me to the dark opening. I hear Keelan's cries behind me, but I don't have enough strength to run to him. The demons drag me into the dark.

I drop to the floor, cold and wet. The bloodied clothes stick to my skin. The air is almost too cold to breathe in. My lungs burn with each breath. My eyes feel as though I have looked at the sun for too long. I am exhausted, I can feel myself drifting into a sleep, and then I snap back to reality.

"Well, that was fun, wasn't it?" The stone door creaks open.

In comes Samael and his demons, all walking in a perfectly straight line. Behind them is Victoria, with her hands bound by rusty chains. Bruises cover her face and hands, but don't look nearly as bad as Keelan or I. Her eyes stay to the ground, with her book in hand. They must have hurt her as well. Her eyes are numb.

"Juliet, you're okay," Victoria shouts. "What happened to you? Where was Keelan?"

The demon escorts her and yanks on her chains, sending her to the floor. She winces in pain. Her wrists are scratched and inflamed from the spikes digging into her skin. The spikes are rendering her of all her magic.

"I am fine. Keelan is fine." I lie.

Samael stands in the middle of the room. A pentagram exactly similar to the one I have on my arm, is burnt into the stone. The torches make the pentagram shift, almost as if it was alive. The demons stand at each point of the star. Victoria and I are on separate sides of the room. We eye each other, both thinking the same thing. There is no way out.

"Juliet, please come." Samael directs.

I hesitate. His hot hands touch my shoulders, and he places me at the top point of the star. He takes one last look at the lineup.

"Perfect," He clasps his hands. "We must begin."

His sinister laugh bounces off the walls. I am frozen in fear, completely clueless as to what is about to happen next. He needed me for a certain task. I don't want anything for him, but I kind of put myself in this situation. I fought so hard to seek him out, not really knowing what I was getting myself into. If I had never met him in Stull, his demons would have caught up to me, eventually. I can't run the rest of my life.

Samael hands me a book bound in black leather. The spine has scales that are almost snake-like. I sit the book down in the middle of the stand and the pages flip to the exact page needed to be at. The page has no pictures. The handwriting was small and almost cursive like. It's barely legible. The language was unfamiliar to me. It was not Latin or anything I could decipher. One word stands out to me, though. Lilith.

"I can't read this," I state.

"Victoria will help you translate." Samael walks to the door we came through. "But just in case you are hesitant, I have a little guest for you."

The door opens and two demons hold a girl in their arms. The blonde hair is all too familiar. My stomach heaves.

"Regina?" I shout. "Why do you have her?"

"I needed to make sure you do what you are told."

Regina struggles beneath the demon's claws. Her eyes are bloodshot. She doesn't look good. Her skin is pale. I wonder how long they have kept her.

"Juliet, where are we? Where have you been? I thought you were dead."

"You are going to be fine, do you hear me? Just stay put and close your eyes."

I honestly thought Samael would never stoop so low to even bring my friends into this. But then again, he is the devil, an angel in disguise. He is manipulative in every way. Now I have no choice but to do as he says, and Regina's life may end before my eyes, and it will all be because of me.

I watch Regina struggle in the hands of the demons. The fear in her eyes makes my stomach turn. This is the kind of magic I never wanted her to see. It's traumatizing for anyone.

Victoria hesitantly comes to my side. We share a look of despair. Her eyes are red and her right eye is black and blue underneath. Samael must have hurt her, too. They probably beat her to get information out of her. Or knowing Samael, he did it all for fun. I could never forgive myself for getting her into this mess. The night we first met, she made it clear that she didn't want to be involved. I don't want her to think I pressured her into helping me.

They bring a small wooden table out beside Victoria and I. On it is a silver chalice, filled with something like wine, a black candle, an incense stick and a rusted knife. The rusted knife startles me, and if this spell required blood, it would be my blood spilled.

The stones open from behind us. Keelan enters the room, dragged by his feet. His body is still bloody from minutes earlier. The demons drop him at the center of the pentagram. He is barely moving anymore. My nerves itch to go to him, but in doing so, I may end up dead. I can't decipher the book to know what is to come. The language is unfamiliar to me. I'm doing this blindly.

"To do this right, we must have an immortal invoke her spirit. Mr. Harrington is the perfect bait," Samael rubs his hands together. "Don't worry though, darling, this will only hurt a lot."

Samael races to me and grabs my stiff hand. The rusted knife somehow ends up in his hands; I didn't see him pick up the knife. He traced the blade down my hand from the left and right of my palm. Blood spilled over my palm and it pooled on the ground. The pain isn't as bad as Keelan devouring my entire arm. Samael dips his hand into my blood. He smears it on Keelan's face. I'm not sure if he was trying to trigger his vampire instincts or not. Keelan is still.

"Right, let's begin."

The spell rolls off her tongue so eloquently, like she has been speaking the language for years.. I repeat the words. Then realize I'm speaking Hebrew. It's rare for a spell to be spoken in Hebrew. Only the unholiest of spells are spoken in Hebrew. And with that knowledge, I fear for my life right now.

"Raise from the ashes of hell."

"I summon thee to roam the earth."

"I release you from your chains of fire."

The temperature drops drastically in a matter of seconds. Victoria and I stand close together, waiting for something to happen. Keelan twitches, almost seizure-like. I grab onto Victoria's fingers, making slight movements so Samael doesn't see me.

The torches lose their orange glow and turn to blue fire, hell fire to be exact, the everlasting fire that tortures the souls who end up in hell. The fire is hotter than regular fire. I feel the sweat rolling down my temples.

"Mother of demons and immortals."

Suddenly Keelan crawls to his feet, as if nothing happened. His face is expressionless, and the blood on his face doesn't bother him. His eyes stare into nothing, almost like he's hypnotized. He doesn't look like himself. It's like his soul has left his body, and he is an open vessel.

The ground bursts beneath Keelan, but he stands unfazed by the rocks flying around him. The demons surrounding us dance, swaying their hips side to side and their gruesome arms above their heads. Their robes dance beneath their feet. The sight is completely horrifying. The magic of the ritual takes over their bodies.

"Juliet, you must know something," Victoria whispers. "Lilith, isn't just the demon of the immortals. She represents lust and sexuality."

My eyes pool with tears. This is why Samael put Keelan in the center of the pentagram. He would not be sacrificed to death; he is bait for Lilith's sexual desires to lure her in. I have no way to undo what has already been done.

A tingly feeling courses through my fingertips and travels down to my thighs and between my legs. The sides of my ribcage ache with a warm sensation; it takes my breath away. The feeling doesn't bother me so much, it's the memory of the feeling that scares me more.

"Just breathe through it," Victoria whispers.

"What was this feeling?"

"It was Lilith. She wants us to submit."

The tingling doesn't subside, but only gets worse. Impure thoughts race through my head. Fantasies of Keelan and I expressing our love intimately. I want to act on it, but I know it is all a trick to the mind. Fantasies of Keelan pass and thoughts of Samael take place. I tell myself to just breathe through these wicked thoughts.

Samael stands by and watches the horror fest. It brings him pleasure to watch us lose control of our senses and our bodies. It's sickening to think he has this kind of control over people. He makes us give in to our desires and deepest fears.

"Let her feast, demon of the night," the demons chant.

Smoke rises from the cracks beneath Keelan. He steps to the side as the smoke gets denser. The smoke begins to form into a slim woman. Before our eyes, a woman stands facing us.. Her naked body is covered by her flowing and matted hair.

She rubs her body against Keelan's, and he is broken from his motionless state. He no longer knows of my existence.. Lilith caresses his body, and Keelan looks into her demon eyes. Her smile is wicked beyond belief. Her snake-like tongue grazes the side of his cheek. She is controlling him without saying a word. She simply uses her beautiful looks and her evil mind.

"I can't watch this," I cry.

"Hush now, dear. We are just getting started," Samael breathes.

Samael finds pleasure in watching others lose complete control of themselves. He knows this is hurting me more than ever. This is something he knew would hurt Keelan and I. He may be the Devil, but he is clever, and smarter than people think. Manipulation and deceit fuel him.

Keelan grabs Lilith's face and pushes her hair behind her ears. He kisses her for what seemed like an eternity. His hands travel along her body. This isn't him. He is being controlled. When will this end?

"When does this end?" I turn to Victoria.

Her eyes are fixed on Keelan and Lilith. I snap my fingers to break her from the trance.

"This has to stop," I rub my arms, "We have to do something."

"It's too late."

I break my eyes from the grotesque scene. All I hear is the crackling of the fire and the moans of the creatures. I can't tune it out. The noise is overbearing. I peer at Samael, he's got an evil smile plastered across his face. Oh, how I wish I could rip that smirk off his face and feed it to him.

"I think we have had enough fun... for now," Samael laughs.

Lilith breaks away from Keelan, and he falls to his knees. Samael opens his arms to Lilith.

"What an entrance, my dear," He hugs Lilith tightly.

"I'm happy to please you, my lord?" Her voice echoes off the walls.

Samael kisses Lilith as if she didn't just have a moment with Keelan. All the while, Keelan is on his knees in the center of the broken pentagram. I hear his silent sobs. Victoria looks at me with terror. I can hear her thoughts. *Don't go to him.*

"I have to."

Samael is occupied. The demons are still and no longer dancing. The torches returned to their original orange glow. Almost everything is still. The portal to hell is sealed, but the monster is standing in front of me.

"Keelan, are you okay?" I kneel beside Keelan.

His sobs become louder. I'm not sure if he can hear me or not. I tap on his shoulder multiple times. Silently, he sits, staring off into the void. His senses are off. He is stuck in his own mind, and I don't know if I can ever get him out.

"Keelan, can you hear me?"

Stones fly through the air as I try to talk to Keelan. Dust surrounds me and blurs my vision. I shield my face from any flying debris. I cover Keelan's body with mine to protect him. He still was unaware of the surroundings.

"Regina, I have to find Regina."

I search around but I can see only the dust that blinds my eyes. I cannot hear her anymore. I can't hear her gentle cries.

I hear screaming off the walls, but they aren't familiar.. Footsteps shuffle around us. I can see the bottoms of the red robes and black shoes encircling us.

"Juliet, there you are," a voice calls.

Bristol comes to my side. Her blonde hair now ashen from the dirt in the air.

"What are you doing here?" I scramble.

"Here to save you."

CHAPTER ELEVEN

"She was beautiful." Bristol holds up the painting. "That was until she became sick. Her skin sunk into her face, her eyes bulged from her skull. It was traumatic."

The old painting is dull in color, and the edges curl up. Scribbled in the corner is the name Katherine Williams, an exquisite young lady with rosy cheeks and blonde hair, just like her children. Bristol and Allister are the spitting image of their mother. It's almost frightening.

"Every morning, she would take us on a walk in the nearby trails. She was never one to be outdoors, but she made sacrifices to make us happy," Bristol smiles.

I love to see Bristol finally opening up to me. When we first met, we didn't get off to a good first start. I thought she would be the type of girl to be self-centered and narcissistic. Maybe she had a change of heart because another girl entered the house, that girl being me.

"Where was this picture painted?" I ask.

"Verona, Italy. One of my favorite places we traveled to. It was one of the richest cities in Europe. We stayed there longer than we should have. People began to suspect us, when many years went by and my father never grew a white hair."

I imagine the Verona breeze hitting my face. I see myself riding through the countryside, bareback on a wild horse, smelling freshly made wine and trees of the spring. I'd do anything to experience the culture and pure happiness Bristol once did.

I have enjoyed the friendship that Bristol has offered me. I love the memories she has shared with me, even if it wasn't easy for her to divulge in her past. I'd certainly be lonely without another girl here to share secrets with and gossip with. The thought of Bristol being the only girl I talk to makes me miss Regina more than ever

When Bristol and the others came to save us from Samael, I realized I could put my trust into this family, especially Bristol. Ever since then, she and I have become closer. We took walks every day, and she told me of all her adventures through the decades. As she described her life, I see it in my head like a movie. I wanted to watch more, but only to take my mind off the actual problems.

Many brave witches sacrificed their lives for Keelan and I. They used their gifts to fight the power of Satan. Arthur had constructed an army of witches and immortals alike. Somehow, Arthur found us and rescued us from the chains of Satan. They weren't able to kill him, only hold him back for a short amount of time. The one good thing about Samael being on earth, is that he doesn't have his full powers in his human body. If he were to return to hell, then he would gain those powers back. He'd only have power here if he took someone's magic.

Satan still lives in this realm. I know this isn't over. He couldn't have waited many years for me to be born just for me to summon his lover. He has something more sinister in the back of his head. I am ready for it. Whatever it is.

It has been a month since I released Lilith. Nothing has happened in the world of immortals. We lived as if Satan did not roam the earth in his human form, with his lover Lilith. They have made no contact, and no strange occurrences have happened since Lilith's soul has come back to Earth.

I haven't seen Edith or made contact for weeks. She probably assumes I am dead. I want to reach out to her, but I feel like I would disappoint her in ways she could never forgive me for. I wouldn't know what to say If I saw her. Either she would greet me with open arms, or deny me. I don't want to find out.

I have lived the past month, isolated from the others. Bristol and I would go on walks once in a while. Arthur did what he had done for the past hundred years. Allister went back to his studies, and Keelan has locked himself in his room, becoming a complete recluse.

I know he's still alive. The maid brings him a glass of blood every day to his door, but not enough to survive on. He doesn't write to me, and he won't answer the door to anyone but the maid. Maybe he is ashamed of what happened, or maybe he feels a certain way toward Lilith and he doesn't have the heart to tell me.

We haven't spoken since then. I long to hear his voice. I just want to clear things between us.

I don't remember the trip back to the house after the ritual. I try so hard to remember any details, but I just can't form them in my head. I make up my own memories, maybe to ease my mind. But one memory that sticks out to me is when we arrived back at the house. Keelan never set an eye on me, he never spoke a word to me. He locked himself in his bedroom without hesitation. I gave him a day to rest, but the days after that meant he didn't want any contact with me or anyone.

Victoria has reconnected with Arthur. She's been coming around more often. I'm not sure what their relationship is like, but when she visits, I can see a new light in her eyes. Her aura is brighter, and the energy surrounding her is more positive. Something still traumatizes her from the ritual. We never talk about it, and I want to keep it that way. We can never talk about it again.

I spend most of my days in my room. It's so tiring seeing the white wooden walls and the single window that shows almost no light. I pace back and forth to keep my blood flowing. I often forget what day it is. Time is no more. Living in this room is making me insane.

I hear footsteps outside my door. I go to it before they have the chance to knock.

"Oh, it's you," I say.

Allister gives a half smile.

"Sorry to disappoint you."

Allister's blonde hair falls over his eyes like he had been running through a tornado. I wondered what crazy contraption he was trying to open this time.

"I have some good news though," He breathes. "Keelan is finally out of his room."

My heart palpitates as I gasp for air. My muscles itch to run to him with all I have in me. I don't know if I should approach him yet, but his state of mind might not be back to normal yet. This is the first time he has been out of his room. I have to see him, whether he wants me to or not.

"Greenhouse," Allister says.

I say nothing more before I skip down the stairs. I have to contain my excitement. I don't want to put Keelan through more than he already had been. I don't want to be clingy, but there are things that were said, kisses stolen, and feelings that won't go away. I need to see him.

I escape out the door. A burst of cold wind makes my eyes water. It is the perfect excuse in case I cry. The grass is now dead and crunchy leaves lie gracefully on the ground. Grey clouds cover the sky, and Birds circle around the house above, talking to each other, their sound traveling through with the wind.

I approach the greenhouse entrance. Arthur walks out of the greenhouse and gently closes the door behind him. It's clear from Arthur's expression that Keelan is not doing well.

"Arthur, is he okay?" I mumble. I know Keelan can hear me. Arthur shakes his head.

"He has gone through a substantial amount of trauma. I fear he may never recover."

It isn't what I want to hear, but it is the truth. What I say next has to be thought through carefully. Keelan is vulnerable in his state, especially sensitive. I can't make it worse. I can't mention Lilith or Samael's name. I don't want to trigger him into another spiral. I have to think before I speak.

"I need to see him. I have to see him with my own eyes." I cross my arms. "I hope you understand."

Arthur nods his head. He opens the door for me and the scent of earth hits me in the face. I know Keelan can sense my presence, and the previous conversation with Arthur.

Keelan is hidden in the jungle of greenery. Plants of all sizes line the walls, perfectly placed in their pots. It's almost like a maze during spring. An array of colors catch my eye, and dark green leaves hang over their pots. The temperature differs from outside. Inside here, the air is musty, full of moisture. Outside, the air is cold enough to kill the plants in one second.

I turn my head at the sound of rustling down the walkway. I peek through the opening in the leaves. I see him. He tends to his plants so gracefully. It's ironic though; he tends to the living while he is dead himself. The dead are not connected to this earth, therefore making it difficult to keep the slightest thing alive.

The plant he rustles with is clearly dead. The leaves are shriveled and faded to a deep brown; they look dry and so fragile. Even the most dainty blow of wind could easily destroy the plant.

"Vivifica," I whisper.

The plant lifts from the ground and becomes upright and more colorful than ever. Leaves begin to turn juniper green and flowers bloom white. The colors are almost blinding compared to the dull grey sky. It's nice to see vibrant colors against the dark colors the winter gives.

I hear a faint chuckle.

"Juliet. Please come out." He sounds happy, but the undertones of his voice say otherwise

I creep around the corner of the aisle. Something about him has changed. I can't quite put my finger on it. His eyes are the same, the redness around his eyes is the same. Maybe it's the way he holds himself. The trauma consumes him, like that is all he has ever been.

"How are you?" I ask. Listening to myself, I realize that may have been the worst question to ask. I'm not good at breaking silence.

"You know," He looks at the plant I revived. "My parents were florists. We owned a shop in Manhattan. We lived right above the shop in a tiny two-bedroom apartment. Every morning, my mother would get up early and water the plants. She called them her children. She even thought talking to them would help them thrive. I miss her more than ever."

"What happened to your family?" I fiddle with my fingers. I slightly feel ashamed of reviving the plant. Magic is almost like a loophole in life. It can be used to get through the hardest times in life, while it can do the simplest things. I use my magic to heal, but healing the plant to him brings back memories of his past life.

"The building next to us was a cafe, it caught on fire in the dead of night. "He turns away from me, wiping his face. "They couldn't get out in time. I escaped by falling three stories onto the concrete."

The events play in my head like a horror movie. I see the many ways his body might have landed, how painful it must have been to land on the cold ground. I could almost hear his bones cracking against the violent fall. I can't fathom the terror in his eyes when he fell on to the ground, looking up to his home encased in fire. My stomach churns at the stark horror.

"What was it like?" I mumble.

He caresses the plant and inhales its scents. He lets the painful memories flow back into him.

"Painful. I suffered in silence and completely alone, all while my family burned to death above me. I was helpless. Arthur found me on the sidewalk, barely holding onto life," He takes a step back from the plants. "He was only passing through, but decided to help me. He changed me into who I am today."

"He saved your life," I cough.

"He made me into a monster. My family raised me to treat life like it would end tomorrow, and now, I take lives to survive. How was that fair?"

He stares into the void. My eyes wander around the greenhouse. I'm not actually looking at the plants, but trying to distract myself from the awkward silence.

"Why do you want me? You can give life, but yet I take it from others? We are complete opposites"

"For life to function the way it does, there has to be opposites. Dark and light, evil and good, even life and death." My cheeks turn red.

I mean, it's true, I want him to always be in my life, maybe as more than friends. I just haven't had the guts to tell him yet.

"I have these feelings for you that I can't describe, but I have felt them before I knew who you really were. Do you honestly think I'd change my mind after everything we have been through?"

He pulls me to him. Our hands intertwine. His cold, familiar breath creeps on my neck. He licks his lips. His breathing becomes harder and faster. I see his fangs creep through the cracks in his lips. Perfectly white, despite all the years of blood spilt onto them.

He pulls up my sleeve to see the scars his teeth had made when under Samael's control. He brushes his fingertips against them. They don't hurt much anymore, but once in a while, pain will radiate off of them.

"I hurt you. I almost killed you, and yet you stay," He breathes.

"That was not you. Samael made you do this. Do not apologize," I lift his chin to meet my eyes, " It seems like you are trying to find reasons to push me away; it won't work."

He kisses me so deeply, more than ever before. I feel myself lift from the ground. "I vow to always protect you, till my dying breath."

"This isn't a wedding, Keelan. I know who you are and what you stand for, and that is all I want."

Keelan chuckles. I finally see him breakthrough. After many days of not seeing him or hearing from him, I wish I had come to him sooner. I should have forced myself through. We had gone so long without communication, it damn near almost killed us both. I sincerely hoped nothing else could set us apart.

***

The front door to the house is open. It is usually shut to keep the air in and the light out. We heard no one approach the house during our conversation. Surely, Arthur and the others knew there was someone inside. Keelan stands in front of me, to guard me from anything or anyone trying to harm us.

As we enter the foyer, we hear talking in the living room down the hall. The floors creak with every step we take. Keelan's hand rests against my thigh to make sure I'm still behind him.

We turn the corner into the living room. Four middle-aged men stand in black suits. Their faces don't have a single wrinkle or any mark to tell how old they really are. But the dark circles under their eyes could tell many stories. Looking into their eyes frightens me, their almost white eyes watching my every move.

"Ahh, Mr, Harrington and Ms. Arden. Lovely for you to finally arrive." The tallest one speaks. "Forgive my manners, I am Elder Henry."

His stiff hands grab mine in a split second, and I have no option but to shake his hand. He caresses the top of my hand and turns over my hand so my wrists are up. He observes the veins flowing through my arm. Keelan stands by, huffing. His eyes have turned black.

"We come bearing some rather harsh news," Henry says.

"Are you taking Juliet?" Keelan blurts.

Henry looks at Keelan with beaming eyes. Keelan shouldn't have spoken out of turn. I'm clueless as to what the Elder's are capable of, but I don't want to disrespect them to find out.

"Things are becoming complicated. We need her for a quick journey," Henry laughs.

"What is so complicated that you need to take Juliet. She doesn't trust you." Keelan insists.

Keelan is right. I don't trust them enough to willingly leave with them. I've Just gotten over the fact that my old friend is a vampire and has been living with vampires. Why did the Elder's think they could just take me without a fight? I'm not an object to be thrown around and used whenever I am needed.

"There have been some unexplained deaths in the vampire communities. Vampires and immortals of every kind are dropping dead everywhere."

It's unheard of for an immortal to suddenly drop dead without being struck by a stake or decapitated by another. The horror in the vampire's faces dims the room. Whether what the Elder's spoke of is true or not, I had to find a solution. If not for them, but to save my friends.

"What do you mean?" I ask.

Keelan shuffles around the parlor, looking through a timeline of books, dates that go back to the fifteen hundreds. His brain is ticking. But I can't quite figure out what was going on inside of his head.

"I'll go with you," I say. "But only for Keelan and the others. If what you say is true. I want to help. I have already done enough damage by summoning Lilith."

Keelan grabs my arm forcefully. His black eyes penetrated my soul.

"Hell no. You aren't going anywhere with them, at least not without me." Keelan exclaims.

"That is out of the question. You two have caused more trouble than World War Two," Henry circles around Keelan and I. "The girl goes with us, or you die."

I hope Keelan will keep his pride to a minimum. I understand why he thinks the way he does, but if he continues on this path of disrespect, we would have no life together. I cannot be with someone who has no self control and no control over their anger. I am already risking my life by being surrounded by blood drinkers.

"If I may cut in," Allister clears his throat. "Juliet summoned Lilith, but only did so because Samael forced her. We must know the reason he wanted Lilith. And if you ask me, Lilith might be the one causing the deaths."

Allister and Bristol look at each other in unison.

"She is the mother of all immortals," Allister walks around us. Keelan hovers over me. "She can make someone immortal, and she can kill them with the snap of her fingers. Lilith would not do this unless Samael demanded her to. The immortal are her children."

"It certainly is a possibility," Henry adds. "We still need the girl. Samael needed her because she is powerful. She may be powerful enough to stop it."

Arthur stood in the room's corner with his arms crossed the entire time. He never even gave his input, but I could tell the gears are moving in his head. He was thinking about something. We waited for one of us to break the silence.

"With all due respect, Henry, would it be possible for my clan to investigate the deaths together?" Arthur emerges from the corner. "I fear separating the love birds will only cause more harm. You told me yourself that you trust me. Please trust me with this task. I will keep them in line."

Henry looks to the other Elders, who have remained quiet the entire meeting. They whisper among themselves. There's no way the other vampires are hearing them, since their faces are all scrunched up. It must have been some type of magic, so other vampires can't hear their conversations.

"I suppose we could arrange that. We would rather not get our hands messy, but if you insist on taking on this task, it is yours," Henry says. "You must keep a close eye on the girl though."

Arthur nods.

The Elder's appear hesitant. They don't want to give Arthur the responsibility of investigating. I wouldn't either, considering Keelan and I have already escaped from the house once. But if it meant I'd be with Keelan longer, we have to take it.

The Elders leave in a hurry. No more is said after Arthur had made the suggestion. As much as I hated vampires, I knew they didn't want to die, either. Who would want to spend their last moments investigating deaths, while waiting for their lives to end as well?

"We are traveling to the nearest vampire coven to get more answers. They have a witch there that witnessed an immortal dying." Arthur pushes past us.

Did every vampire coven have a witch living with them? As if they aren't already powerful enough, they just needed the icing on the cake, a witch, to fix all their problems. Now I feel like I was only here to do what the vampires could not. I didn't want to be used.

"Keelan, you are staying here, with Allister," Arthur says.

"No. You just said Juliet and I shouldn't be separated," Keelan screams. "How could you go back on your word?"

"I told them what they wanted to hear."

"No. I'm going. There is no discussion on this."

Allister and Bristol look at each other and snicker. The way Keelan has been behaving embarrasses me. He's being overly protective. I know he loves me, but how can he think acting that way would be good for anyone?

"Fine," Arthur says. "But if anything happens while we are there. I will kill you myself."

We pack immediately for the long trip. I stuff sweaters and socks into the side pocket of the duffle bag. Bristol was kind enough to loan me extra clothing, since I didn't have mine. Her style was surely eccentric and definitely not my style. But, clothes are clothes.

We're going to a small town secluded in Maine. I long to see the snow atop the dead trees and the soaring mountains. I have never been so far up north. It almost feels like a vacation to me. I almost had forgotten the last time I actually went on a relaxing vacation. I was ten when my aunt took me to a church camp. Aside from having mass every day, I had a pretty good time.

The door creaks open. I finish filling the bag and push the lid down to zip it.

"Hey," Keelan emerges from the doorway. "Can I talk to you for a second?"

"Sure." I hear the uncertainty in his voice.

"This coven is not like ours. They are not so good at controlling themselves."

I imagine a feral vampire smelling my scent through the air and ripping my throat out. Surely Keelan would never let it happen, and maybe that was why he wanted to come. Victoria and I will be the only witches there, besides the one who lives in the coven. The woman had to have some type of control over the strength of the vampires. Otherwise, she'd be dead.

"I'll be fine."

Arthur has other plans for transportation, but Bristol tells him about the car hidden in the trees. He isn't angry with their lack of honesty, but it's better than the train he wanted to use. A train would have been too public. They'd stand out in a crowd.

The further we travel north, the icier the terrain becomes. The roads are slick, and patches of ice hide within the cracks. Allister's driving is not the best. Arthur looks incredibly uncomfortable in the passenger seat. Keelan, Bristol, and I can't help but laugh at Arthur's uneasiness. At least we can laugh about something amongst the stress.

We try to make the best out of the ride. Keelan and I thumb wrestle like we used to on the bus, but he had an advantage over me with his vampire strength, which isn't fair. Once in a while we would play I spy, Arthur never understood silly human games. Victoria and I snack on junk food almost the whole way there while the vampires sip blood from their cups, as if we didn't know what is in them. I'm constantly wiping blood from the corner of Keelan's mouth although I'm still not okay with his blood drinking.

We travel along a long back road for miles. I lost track of time. I fell in and out of sleep. I dream of nothing, at least from what I remember there was only a black void and Keelan's soothing voice in my ear. I believed he had some kind of mind control, and he prevented the nightmares I usually have. Usually I'd become car sick falling asleep in a car, but I think my anxiety prevented that from happening.

I try not to think of the mission at hand, but my mind keeps wandering to the worst potential scenarios. I keep thinking about the Elders and what their jobs really are. So far, I've noticed they're only around when someone breaks rules of some kind. They haven't punished anyone while I was living in the house. Atleast to my knowledge They are kind of like the vampire police.

"The Elders have been around for centuries. They come from many backgrounds including Buddhism, paganism and even Christianity. Their job is to keep peace within the immortal realm.

Though not always easy, sometimes they have to kill to keep the peace." Keelan explains.

"They are religious? I would have never thought."

Keelan nods.

"What's even more weird, is that their bodies are not their own," Keelan looks out the window. "They are souls possessing a mortal body."

"Keelan, that is enough. Do not scare the poor girl." Bristol shouts.

"She has dealt with more vampires than witches in her life. I think it is time she knows what she is dealing with."

Their bickering becomes nothing but white noise. The Elders only possess bodies of the mortal. They have the ability to become whomever they want to at any given time. That has to be some type of ancient magic. I've never heard of it, but it sounds dangerous.

"So the current deaths that are happening leave them unaffected?" I ask.

"Yes. Once their physical body dies, they can move on to the next one. It's called soul jumping."

The Elders could have done the investigation the whole time. Maybe that's why they agreed so quickly to allow Arthur to take the lead. The Elders are untouchable. It's so cruel to do this to their own kind.

Victoria reaches into her bag and pulls out a small journal. It's held together by a small string. I don't ask what it is, I only assume it's something I need to read. Upon opening it, small words are scribbled into it. It's almost too small to read.

Soul jumping: a skill in which an individual, magical or non-magical, may jump from mortal body to mortal body. Said individual cannot reuse a body once they have left it completely. Once the mortal body dies, the soul will automatically transfer to the next available host.

"So the mortal bodied person has no say in who takes over their body?"

"Exactly," Keelan responds.

"What are the criteria for becoming a host?"

"The person has to have attempted suicide in the past year. If they no longer care about living, then that makes them the perfect host."

"That is beyond cruel." I hand the journal back to Victoria.

I try to erase the subject of the soul jumpers from my mind. But I already know I am going to be asking questions later on.

We follow a road lined with dead trees. There is a small house spotted in the distance. It's like the one Keelan lives in, but much bigger. The house looks like a smaller version of the White House, only this one was dull with color and has a haunting appearance. Vines encase the house in a green mess. Paint chips off the siding, leaving the original wood uncovered. I wondered how long this house had been on this property.

"Stay in the car," Keelan says.

Everyone but me exits the car, and I am left alone. I am frightened at the sight of a barren and snowy ground. What creature could be lurking around these grounds? What made it so safe for Victoria to go with the group and not me? What power did she have that I did not?

They stand on the porch, waiting for entry. Keelan looks back at me. I wave awkwardly. I see the door open, and they disappear into the dark. After all that I have been through, I'd think I wouldn't fear a monster under a bed, but this moment terrifies me. I've only just recently discovered the existence of vampires, and now I was amid feral vampires; ones that aren't so good at self control.

I hear a buzzing. The seats vibrate. At first I think of just letting it ring, but my mind eats me alive and I have to know who was calling. I cannot just sit here and wait for something to happen.

Victoria's purse is wedged between the door and seat. I shuffled through the mess of a purse and finally found the phone. I feared at any moment the phone would stop ringing and I'd miss the call. The area code was unfamiliar.

"Hello?" I whisper.

Static rings through the phone. An uneasy feeling settles in my stomach.

"Ahh, Juliet. Just the person I was hoping would pick up."

A woman's voice, so soft and eerie, echoes through the phone. I sit in silence, stuck on what to say next. I know the familiar raspy voice.

"Lilith," I breathe. "What do you want? How did you get this number?"

"It wasn't hard to figure out," she laughs. "After all, I know where my immortal children are at all times."

I keep eyeing the front door. I don't know what I'd do if Keelan came back. I couldn't just hang up on a demon. I didn't want to piss her off and definitely didn't want to drive her to do something more rash than what was already doing.

"No matter what you do, Juliet, you can't stop this." the static returns. "Soon, your boyfriend will be dead. Everything immortal will be gone from this world. It is all in Samael's plan Samael."

She insinuates the death of Keelan, along with Arthur, Bristol and Allister. The thought of them no longer being on this earth terrifies me. I've gotten to know each one of them in different ways, and they all have affected my life, good and bad. If what Lilith says is true, I cannot take this lightly anymore. She has set me off.

"So what are you going to do after they are all dead?" I ask.

"I am not going to do anything. This is all for Samael." I hear laughing in the background. "He has a bigger plan for the world. The angels will fall and so will you."

The line clicks on the other end. Just as the tone rings through the phone, Keelan and the others exit the house. I stuff the phone back into the bottom of Victoria's purse. I do the best I can to rub off the finger prints and replicate the way it laid before. I've never felt so guilty. It feels like I've stolen money out of an adult's purse.

The others approach the car. Keelan opens the door and ushers me to exit. His face is full of dismay. Something isn't right, everyone's body movements prove so.

"What's going on?"

Keelan crosses his arms. His eyes wander left and right, searching for the right words to say.

"Well, it's not good. The vampire that died was one of the oldest in the coven. We believe they are dying in the order of age. Oldest to youngest."

That makes sense. I see the terror in Keelan's eyes. If we don't stop this fast, he will surely die for sure. I can't bear the thought of him not walking this earth. I contemplate telling him who I spoke to on Victoria's phone. I am scared he would be angry with me, or even Victoria would be angry with me for invading her belongings.

"How old was the vampire that died?"

"He was five hundred sixty-one, born in the year 1452." Keelan peeks behind me to the others surrounding the car. He knows they can hear our conversation. At this point, I don't know why he bothered to speak quietly anymore.

I don't want to ask the question. I don't want to hear the answer, but after so long of him keeping secrets from me, he had to tell me.

"How old are you, Keelan? Please tell me." My heart sinks deeper into my chest.

"One hundred thirteen years old."

I am somewhat relieved. He's not nearly as old as the vampire who died. We have time to figure this out and put a stop to it. But who knows, the deaths could double in hours or minutes and soon enough Keelan the others will be dead, along with me.

"There are other vampires I care about, Juliet." Keelan eyes Arthur, Bristol, and Allister.

I know he cares about the people who practically raised him. I don't blame him for worrying about their life. Arthur saved him and made him into the person he is today. Arthur has taught Keelan years of knowledge that no other person could learn in one year. Keelan never asked to be saved. Arthur saved him, out of the kindness in his own heart.

"We will stay here for the night," Keelan whispers. "But they don't want you staying in the house. They don't trust the newer vampires not to kill you. They said we can stay in the guest house."

Keelan points to a dainty building in the east. It is isolated from the rest of the vampires. It was no bigger than a roadside gas station. The windows are boarded up, but the paint looks brand new.

"You said we."

Keelan nods his head.

"Both of us?"

"Yes, you think I would leave you to fend for yourself from a bunch of feral vampires?" He says.

Having to share a room with a vampire who doesn't sleep makes me a little nervous. He never sleeps, and his senses are heightened to the point he can hear the blood pumping through my veins, making me the perfect prey. I welcome the idea of sharing a room with Keelan, but I also don't fully trust him, only because of his impulses. I keep telling myself I will be okay, but it only makes me believe it less the more I say it.

The others are welcomed into the house, Victoria as well. She is a mortal witch, just like me, so I don't understand how they let her in, and not me. I now doubt everything Keelan told me about them not wanting me in the house. I feel he made up this lie to protect me, or to get me alone.

The one bedroom guest house is a sight for sore eyes. A single bed sits in the corner of the room, neatly made and quite dusty. A couch is on the other side of the room, a small kitchenette, and a small bathroom by the entrance. The carpet is shaggy, just like from the seventies. I light an incense to rid the place of negative energies and the musky smell.

I rummage through my mess of a bag. I pull out warm socks and sweatpants to go over the ones I am already wearing. No vampire would need a heating system, so there isn't one in the house. Keelan is unbothered by the cold weather.

Keelan stares out the one window that isn't boarded up. I want to know what was going through his head. I try not to think so much, in fear he might read my mind, but that was all fantasy.

"What's going through your head?" I ask.

The moonlight shines off his pale skin. His features shine brighter than they ever have before. I can see him, and I can see the person I used to know. He is more beautiful than ever. I hate myself for never noticing his beauty until now.

"Only things I cannot control," He shifts his weight from one leg to the other. "Immortal problems."

I take offense to that. He implies that this is also not my problem. He is so wrong. We are in this situation because of me. I summoned Lilith. I brought her into this world under the control of Samael. Everything is my fault. *It is always my fault.*

I meet him at the window. I run my hand from his shoulder to his hand. Our fingers find each other's and collapse into another's. He turns to me, and his eyes glow in the light. I rest my hand on his chest. It feels the same as the first time I felt his chest, empty. I raise his hand to my chest. He closes his eyes and focuses on the thumping of my heart. A smile cracks through the corner of his mouth.

"I miss this feeling," He mumbles.

"This feeling doesn't keep me alive," I say.

Although it sounds awkward coming out of my mouth, it is the truth. It feels like my heart beating isn't enough to keep me alive. It may keep my physical body alive, but emotionally, mentally, and spiritually, Keelan keeps me grounded. I can't imagine anyone else going to the ends of the earth with me..

"Listen, there is something I need to tell you."

"Not now. Don't ruin this moment," He presses his finger to my lips.

I want to tell him about the phone call from earlier. It's eating at me, as if it would just roll off my tongue at any moment. I hate keeping secrets from him, or really anyone. It seems so easy for him to do, like he has no conscience. I mean he kept one big secret from me for years. I hope he can't sense my vibrations.

"If I am going to die, I need to leave this world knowing I made you happy."

"You do make me happy. What are you saying?"

He smiles.

"I love you." He takes my hand in his. " And I know you know that, I just want you to hear it from me. I'm not usually the one to let down my guard, but since meeting you, that is all I have ever done. Being so vulnerable is not one of my strong suits."

He leads me to the bed beside us. I sit close to him, never taking my eyes off him. I go back to our earliest memories. The first time we met. It was my freshman year. I had no clue what I was doing or where I was going. The hallways were too maze-like to navigate for a first time high schooler. I hadn't seen Regina yet, she was probably running late.

After trying to find all of my classes before the bell rang, I came across the library. No one but the librarian and I were there. It was so peaceful, almost nothing could be heard from outside the room. I didn't want to leave. I enjoyed the presence of the never ending shelves of books.

I went down almost each aisle, carefully keeping a list of books that I wanted to read. I was stopped in my tracks when I turned down the last aisle. Keelan sat crossed legged on the floor, with his nose hidden in a book I didn't recognize. His hair fell over his face, like it usually does.

He looked up to me and instantly smiled. I probably turned red, I remember feeling my face burn. I couldn't deny he was so cute. Any girl would have fallen for him. He could have been playing football or skateboarding on the sidewalk, but he was in the library reading a book, enjoying the company of the books, same as me.

The moment we laid eyes on eachother, I knew we would be friends in some way. But it never crossed my mind to even be in love with him. I let myself fall for him over the years. We have always been friends, up until now, I think we may be more than that. I gave in to him. So many times I pushed the thought of him away. I can't subdue those thoughts anymore.

"Juliet, say something please. Don't leave me hanging."

I snap out of my trance and regain my focus on Keelan

"I love you too."

His hand tightens around mine, but just enough for me to notice.

"You do?"

I lean in for a kiss, and he pulls me closer to him. Our lips never leave each other's for no more than a few seconds. I never thought I'd welcome the coldness of his lips. I despised everything he is and now I'm confessing my love to him.

Our kiss is broken by a loud bang on the door. A minute passes by and the door flies open. Keelan stands up in front of me. Allister stands in the doorway, hands shaking.

"Another vampire is dead."

CHAPTER TWELVE

"How old was he?"

"Five hundred exactly."

The numbers are going down drastically. They are dying faster than we can crack the code. I'm more scared than I was when we first arrived here. Everyone's faces have changed, and no one seems to throw any ideas out. Everyone is clueless.

Arthur looks at his children. The love in his eyes shines, and it's a part of him I have never seen before. I don't think anyone has, not even Victoria. After years of adventures and travels, Arthur's life is coming to an end. I think he worries more about his children's lives than his own. Any father would. I only wished my own father was here with me.

I have to tell them about the phone call with Lilith. The message she gave me was haunting. But maybe the others had ideas about what to do.

"There is something I need to tell you all," I blurt.

Everyone's eyes are upon me. My cheeks are on fire.

"Yesterday, while I was waiting in the car. Victoria's phone rang, and I answered it."

Victoria looks at me with disappointment. She hurries to her purse and shuffles through it. I don't want her feeling like I have possibly stolen something, but I know she can't help feeling that way. I invaded her personal belongings. Curiosity got the best of me, and I'm glad I answered when I did.

"It was Lilith."

The look of horror spreads across their faces. I don't know if they believe me or not.

"She's tracking all of us. She told me, ``Angels will fall and so will I."

"What is that supposed to mean?" Bristol asks.

"The end of the world perhaps," Keelan exclaims. "No, really think about it. Satan gets power from people dying. Imagine the power he can gain from immortals dying under the hands of Lilith."

Bristol nods. Allister rolls his eyes in annoyance; the all knowing Allister couldn't even crack the code.

"A war is what he wants," Arthur adds.

"A holy war."

I may not have paid much attention in bible study, but I know enough to know the book of Revelations is quite horrifying. Most of it is spoken in metaphors. Its apocalyptic literature contains the most detailed version of how the world was supposed to end, but none of it talks about immortals dying in the hands of Lilith. It doesn't even mention her in the Bible. None of the immortals are. So this makes little sense.

" In the book of Revelations, it talks about the end times. Those who practice magic, the murderous, the sexually immoral and the unbelieving will spend an eternity in the lake of fire. That is the second death."

I never really believed that the witches would go to hell. A majority of us don't see Samael as a threat to us. Although we gain most of our power from Lilith, we also obtain our power from mother earth. This is this side of witchcraft I'd rather live by. To me, it seems like the more moral practice. I'm at a crossroads when it comes to magic and the devil. God says I am sinning, but I believe differently. It's how you use your magic.

Victoria's eyes become full of tears. Something must have clicked inside her head. She holds back though. Her eyes move away from mine. She wipes her face with the edge of her sweater.

"My sister used to recite that verse all the time. She knew so much about the book of revelations, it was almost frightening." Victoria cries.

"I'm so sorry Victoria. Did your sister pass away?"

"Not exactly. We went our separate ways." She sniffs. " It doesn't matter now. We have to get to the bottom of this."

Bristol huffs in the background. "Okay, I'm sorry to hear that but how does that information help us?

I want to slap Bristol so far into next week she would never remember what happened. I don't understand how she could be so caring, then completely turn around the next second. I don't care if we are in a situation. Victoria is hurting and I was only trying to help.

"Don't you see? He is trying to kill us all now, to gain power to defeat God."

"Wasn't God trying to kill all wicked things in the Bible, anyway?" Keelan asks.

"You're right. But when an immortal is made, a piece of Lilith's soul is given to that person for their supernatural abilities. He is using Lilith as a weapon to destroy God."

I'm angry that I never knew this. Then again, I didn't have a proper teacher to teach me about the witch community and history. All of this is new to me. I'm learning things I should have known years ago. I shouldn't be angry with Edith for withholding such information, but I know she was only trying to do what was best for me. Maybe she thought if I didn't know anything, then I couldn't cause more harm. The thought is ridiculous.

We all stand in silence as we put the pieces together. This all makes sense. This has to be the reasoning behind the deaths of the vampires. If that's the case, then I will soon die as well, but my soul will be in the hands of Satan.

"If you all die. Victoria and I die too. Eventually. All the witches will. That is where most of our power comes from." I add.

Keelan pinches the bridge of his nose. A tear drops to his cheek, but wipes it before anyone can notice. He knows he could not be weak in this situation. He may be full of emotion but one side of him tells him to hide it at all costs, as if feeling emotion is a sign of being weak.

"So how do we stop her?" Bristol asks.

"We don't."

Two vampires exit the house and make their way to us. Keelan stands in front of me, but I take a step to the side.

There is a big difference in height between the vampires. One was much taller than the other by a few feet. The woman's face is pale, just like Keelan's, but her eyes are jet black. She has dark circles under her eyes and dresses as if she still lives in the year she was born. Her lips quiver as she stares at my neck. The male vampire towers over her like a building. His eyes are black as well. He purses his lips and positions his body facing away from me.

"We can still smell the girl. I think it's best if you all return to your rooms if you do not plan on leaving." He speaks in an accent I can't quite figure out. It sounds similar to russian, but not quite.

The woman standing next to him inhales discreetly to catch the scent of my flesh. I no longer feel safe out in the open. I squeeze Keelan's hand, trying not to draw attention to myself. Maybe If I don't move, my scent won't be as potent.

"We have figured it out," Arthur says.

The vampires listen in on the conversation from earlier about the book of Revelations and the prophecy of a holy war. They nod their heads in agreement, but it saddens them at the thought of no solution.

"I'm sorry to hear that." The woman smirks. "Guess we will have to live our lives to the fullest before our departure. Such a shame."

She spoke as if she just didn't care about her life anymore. She had to have been hundreds of years old. Being alive for that long would seem monotonous, and I wouldn't want to live anymore. Doing the same thing everyday would be so tiring, and mentally exhausting.

They leave in silence. I'm sad at the thought of being so helpless to them. One day they are living their lives and the next they are being picked off one by one. Despite their uncontrollable mannerisms, I still felt great sadness for all of them.

Keelan and I return to our room. We say nothing to each other as I lay in the bed where we once shared a moment. We are both too disappointed to say anything. I'm not sure if I could lighten the mood. I want to be able to talk to him with no problems, but I know we are both too depressed to form words.

I have to think of ways to fix this. This can not be the end of an entire race. The vampires have seen things and experienced things humans could not. Their knowledge is above anyone else's. They feel differently, physically and emotionally. Despite their savage behavior and thirst for blood, I consider them superior to humans.

I relive all the events over the past few weeks. I go over each situation, piece by piece, pausing them like a movie, and deconstructing it to dig further. Some things make sense, and others make no sense at all. I am frustrated. I only wish Edith was here to be with me through it all.

I miss her, and I can honestly say that now. I can't help but wonder if she would ever find out if I was dead. The thought of her never knowing crushes me. Would they find my body, rotting in an unknown location? The opposite would be just as bad; they will never find my body. Edith would never get the closure she deserves.

I also miss Regina. I haven't been able to speak to her. She could be dead for all I know. Samael used held her for ransom just to force me to do the ritual. I couldn't find her after Bristol found us. I can't imagine coming home to find her dead. She knew nothing of what this world was like; she is such a pure soul. It tears me apart.

I remember the first time we met. Elementary school was rough for me. I had just started a new school and no one liked me, but she took an interest in me on the first day. I still see the green turtleneck and bell-bottom jeans she wore so vividly. She would never be caught wearing such a thing now that she is older. Her blonde hair curled under and tickled her face. To others she was only a bully, but to me she treated me like her own child.

Never in my life would I have ever thought my parents are a witch and an angel. It just doesn't seem real to me. Any regular person would have witches for parents or be normal. I got the crappy end of the stick. I'd never see Esther again, and I don't know how I'd be able to talk to my father. I will soon go to hell, and if he was an angel, we would be on two different sides of the vale. Two sides that are forbidden to ever make contact with each other.

If my father is an angel, then I must have some sort of angelic abilities. I know I can summon and banish beings, and because of that ability, Lilith is now killing every immortal in the world. I don't know if there is any other gift I may have besides those two.

I got it. I have the ability to summon and banish. If I can get to Lilith without Keelan knowing, I could banish her back to hell. I don't even know where to start. I couldn't track her, and I'm sure she wouldn't want me following her. She would take every precaution to make sure no one finds her. This mission will be damn near impossible. Keelan wont let me out of his sight.

Chapter Thirteen

The next morning, I feel a great amount of anxiety. My hands cannot stop trembling, and my heart flutters for a few minutes. I'm becoming anxious with the thought of possibly finding a solution, but to get to that part, I'd have to risk my life and leave Keelan and the others. If Lilith was killing immortals, no doubt she wouldn't kill him on sight.

"What's going on with you?" Victoria asks. She cups her hands around a steaming mug of green tea.

"I can't talk here."

Her eyebrows crease. She looks around. Keelan and the others stand behind the car planning out their next move.

"Hey, we are going on a walk, alright?" Victoria slings her bag over her shoulder.

Keelan stomps towards us. His eyes are heavy with concern.

"I got this, Keelan. I won't let anything happen to her," Victoria commands.

Keelan reluctantly returns to Arthur and the others. His eyes meet mine and I mouth, "I'm okay." He knows I am not okay.

Victoria and I walk west of the house, through the snow. The trees are barren, but give enough shield to hide us from the rest. I want to be as far away as possible so I can speak freely, without the prying ears of the vampires. I don't know how far they can hear, so I'm not taking any chances.

We stop at an old wooden bridge; it is covered in snow and creeks beneath our feet. Rocks and a tiny frozen stream cross below us. I look around for any signs of people or vampires. I am not sure if they could hear me, but I have to tell Victoria in the most hushed tones.

"So, last night I was thinking," I whisper. "If I am a summoner, witch, I can also banish. My dad was an angel, so that would give me some sort of power, wouldn't it?"

Victoria crosses her arms, "Good thinking. It's possible, but not certain. If you are part angel and part witch, there is no telling what abilities are passed down to you."

I never knew I was part angel until a few weeks ago. Since then, and pretty much since I was born, I've used my magic from Esther's side. I never had the chance to test any of my abilities, except the power to summon. I have to try anything at this point.

"I have to try something."

"Well, to start, we would need to figure out what type of angel your father was. Obviously if he was living here on earth, he must have been working directly with god."

"Archangels. They live on earth as humans."

"Great, I can do some research when we head back home."

"No, we have to do something now. We don't have time." I cry. My hands form into fists.

She will never realize how important this is to me. She's been on this earth longer than I have, so she has lived her life. She has found love and been through so many adventures, the good and the bad.. I have only started living my life, and I have found love. All of it will soon be taken away from me. I have to do something now.

"I need to find Lilith," I kick the snow. "Surely you have a tracking spell somewhere in there."

She flips through the pages, her eyes moving quickly down the pages. She stops at a page and shows me the book. She writes in an unfamiliar language, and I'm not very fluent in Latin. I can only decipher some words. A few words stand out to me: Dream, travel and minute.

"So I have to astral project," I rub my head. "I have never done that before."

"Neither have I, but we can try it. It's risky though."

"And sending me to hell wasn't? I'll take my chances." I give back the book to Victoria. "Come on, let's try it."

I lay down in the snow, making myself the perfect snow bed. It's soft but cold. Laying in the snow makes cuddling with Keelan feel so much better with his cold skin.

"Here? Now? Are you crazy, Arthur and Keelan will come looking."

I lift my head.

"Victoria just do it."

The instructions have to be done precisely. One mess up and all of this could go south. I inhale and exhale many times before closing my eyes. I try to get myself into a meditative state. I look to the treetops and hope to see the light of day again.

I feel light, almost like a feather, but my body is still attached to the ground. My nerves tingle up and down my body. I can hear Victoria's voice go in and out of it. My consciousness is slowly fading from reality.

I think of Lilith's long orange hair flowing over her face and down her body. It covers her from head to toe. Her voice comes to mind, her raspy and devilish-like voice. Her fingers dragging across Keelan's body flashes through my mind. I want to stop, but I have to remember every detail of her, even the bad ones.

I open my eyes and I'm surrounded by floating colors, almost like a rainbow of smoke. I hear sounds I have never heard before. They almost whisper- like, but also screaming. I feel numb all over my body. My hands look almost transparent. I can see the veins inside my skin. When I move, it almost seems as if I am lagging in a video game. This reality is unearthly. No wonder people die being in here too long.

I have a minute to find Lilith. I picture her face and I float into the air. I see the trees below me, and further down I see Keelan and the others huddled around the car. Keelan looks angry. He throws his hands into the air. He walks in the forest direction. He's now looking for Victoria and I.

"Sequantur, Lilith."

I am catapulted to a castle-like wall, light passing by me in flashes. The stones that hold it together reach higher than I can see over. I run down the wall, and find towers, each with one window. A cross is etched into stone on the tallest tower. Under the cross, St. Joan Convent is written on a gold plaque.

I peek through a clear part of a stained glass window. I rest my hands on it and I fall completely through the window. I gasp and hold onto my chest, then remember I am only in spirit form. Things could go through me and I won't feel a thing. I look at this as an advantage.

I follow the loud rumbling through the hallway. It's almost too dark to see where I'm going, but I trust the spell to guide me to where I need to go. I trust Victoria to get me out of here alive.

I pass through the double doors like a ghost. A pit of fire greets me at the door, and luckily I feel no heat radiating from it. Lilith, Samael and their demons stand around the fire, perfectly uniform.

"Why can't we just kill them all now?" Lilith pouts.

"Calm, my love, they must be the last to die."

Lilith stomps around the fire, balling her fists like she wants to strike him. Her infatuation with him is sickening. One minute she bows to his presence, and the other she demands to be the queen. Her biggest flaw is her demon attitude.

"Don't you see, they will find us. They are no match for our power. Besides, you made them, you can easily take their magic."

Samael rubs Lilith's shoulders. She rolls her neck from side to side. She turns around and looks at him with lustful eyes. They embrace with a passionate kiss. I have to turn my eyes from this horrendous scene.

"Do you feel that?" Lilith asks.

Samael looks around, dumbfounded.

"I sense someone was watching us," She hisses.

She lifts her nose to the air, as if trying to track someone like a dog. She must know I'm here spying on them. I have to escape quickly. I have to leave before she pulls me through the vale. I would be lost without my physical body. And if my consciousness doesn't return to my body soon, it will die.

My vision becomes distorted, almost like a glitch in a video game. I'm losing the energy to stay in this state of matter. The fog turns into different shades of grey, losing its vibrant colors. I have to get back to my body before my heart gives out. I cannot die like this. I can't leave everyone behind.

"Reditus."

I wait for myself to return to Victoria, but I am still in the astral state and I am still here. The colors fade in and out of vibrance.

"Reditus," I shout.

If I could feel my heart, it would be racing now. I can't remember the page of the grimoire to know what to do in a situation like this. I know I've been in there longer than a minute. I worry about what is happening in the physical world. What is Victoria thinking, and what is she doing to help me?

I have to get out of here before they find me. I can't imagine being stuck here, or even dying in this state.

I note my surroundings, although I found it harder to concentrate now that all the color is gone. My hearing is becoming muffled, and I can't hear the birds chirping in the forest surrounding the convent.

There are no nuns present inside or outside the abbey. It has been deserted for what seems like years. The bushes in the garden are dead, and the flowers drop to the ground. To me they had no color. The grass is a lighter shade of grey, so I assume it's dead and brown. The windows leading into the convent are dusty and full of spider webs, such a haunting scene.

"Juliet, wake up."

A voice echoes through the sky. I search for any sign of humans, but I know it would be near impossible.

"Juliet, please, wake up."

I realize the voice calling out is Keelan's. I shouldn't be able to hear any voices unless I was on the brink of death. I had to get back now.

"Reditus, Reditus, Reditus!"

I gasp for air, and the cold icy air burns my lungs as it enters me. I cough profusely, almost vomiting on myself. Keelan and

Victoria kneel beside me, their eyes wide and teary. My hands tremble as I reach for Keelan's hand. I need to feel him, to know I am actually back in the real world.

"Juliet, your heart stopped beating for an entire minute," Keelan cries with my hand against his face. "I kept trying to bring you back to life. I thought you were surely dead."

No wonder why my chest hurt so bad. He kept pushing on my chest to restart my heart. I hunch over and focus on my breathing. My muscles relax and my heart slows down at its regular pace. I can feel myself come back to this reality, but it's still disorienting.

"The feeling... was unreal," I whisper.

"You could have killed yourself."

I want to tell him of my adventures, and everything I had experienced; the colorful hues and floating in the air. It was an unimaginable feeling to the regular human, and especially dangerous to the inexperienced like me.

Keelan pulls me to his body and squeezes. Arthur, Bristol and Allister come sprinting through the snow. They all stop and circle around Keelan I. To my surprise, they aren't out of breath. They are unfazed by the physical movements.

"What in the world is going on?" Arthur demands.

Keelan lifts me to my feet, and I catch my balance. I sift the snow off me, my clothes are now drenched from laying down for too long. I can barely feel the skin on my back. I am so cold.

"I know where Lilith is," I pant. "Saint Joan's Convent back in Massachusetts."

"I hope you aren't planning to go there," Keelan snaps.

I want to tell all of them the truth. I want to tell them how I plan to destroy Lilith. I know they won't be the most accepting of my plan, especially Keelan, with his chivalrous acts of protection lately. He, out of all people, cannot know my plan. I may trust Victoria, but the others are untrustworthy. I can't have anyone holding me back.

"I just had to know." I lie through my teeth.

Keelan's eyes are unsure. He runs his eyes across my body, scanning for any signs I may be lying. I stand completely still, almost holding my breath. But he can detect that.

"And what do you plan to do with that information after almost killing yourself?" He crosses his arms. His voice is stern.

"I told you, solely for informational purposes, in case we might need it later," I exhale. "Besides, I could have been wrong. Why would she be hiding in a convent? It's been blessed and deemed a holy place."

Keelan nods. But he's still unsure of my excuse. He turns away from me.

Snow cracks in the distance. The two vampires from earlier trudge through the snow with a desperate look on their face. Their eyebrows crease.

"Don't tell me, another one is dead," Keelan moans.

"Actually, no, but we suspect death is upon him soon. A vampire has fallen ill with a fever."

The vampires turn to each other in disbelief. It's unheard of for a vampire to develop a fever. They are cold creatures. Their body stops functioning like a human the minute they become vampires. Technically their bodies are dead. They have no immune system, and they can heal themselves, so having a fever is life threatening and clearly a new strategy for Lilith to kill them off. She wants us to suffer before our death. Our maker wants us to suffer.

"Let us see him," Victoria states.

"Of course, but the girl still cannot come inside," the male vampire pleads. "With our vampires on edge we still think it's best not to trigger their frenzy."

I fall behind the group to the house. Keelan walks in front of me as if I don't exist. He doesn't look back, and I don't dare make conversation with him. He's truly angry with my selfish and reckless behaviour. I feel it in my gut he can sense that I was lying earlier.

"Stay here," Keelan says without turning to me. "I'll be back soon."

I'm alone in the car with nothing but trees and snow. The icy wind glides across my face, chilling me to the bone. I'm tired of being left in the dust. It's my fault the vampires can't control themselves. They can control themselves just fine with Victoria and their coven's witch around.

A risky thought crosses my mind. I open the door to the Mercedes. The keys are in the ignition. What vampire would be this careless to leave keys inside the car? Probably Arthur, but he's only driven a few times in his life. I go back and forth between the keys and the front door to the house. *Don't do it. Don't be stupid.*

No, I can't do this. I can't possibly leave them here without transportation. Do I really think I could get away with stealing the car? I'm not some thug on the streets stealing a car just to sell it for parts. I can't risk anyone else's lives. Edith would think I am more above this idea. I cannot stoop to a thief's level. I can't give in to the evil that Esther made me into. I cannot prove my wickedness anymore than I have. They cannot know what I plan to do. I have to keep telling myself this is all for their protection.

This curse that follows me, has to end. This evil that surrounds the ones I love cannot be on this earth anymore. I need to leave, for the sake of my friends.

As I look at the house one final time, I am overcome with emotion. No one exists in the house. It's completely still. Once they hear the car turn on, I will have no time to waste. I have to book it out of here and leave. No looking back. I'm becoming nervous at the thought of leaving Keelan behind. How could he possibly forgive me for this?

I search for a paper and pen. The least I could do is leave a note. I scribble on the neon notepad and set it beside the car on the ground. Hopefully, someone will see it against the snow. If not,

Keelan will go to the ends of the earth to find me, even if that means killing others who get in his way.

I buckle the seat belt and observe all the mirrors. I rest my foot on the brake, ready to put it into gear. I start the car and a low mumble rattles the car. I press on the brake and put the car into drive. I stomp on the gas, and the wheels spin beneath me, running onto the concrete road.

In a matter of seconds, I go from zero to sixty. I glance at the mirror, Keelan and the other race out of the house. But they are too baffled to run after me. My heart breaks more than it ever has before. I can't comprehend the amount of heartbreak I'm causing Keelan right now.

CHAPTER FOURTEEN

KEELAN

"What is she doing?" I run out of the house. "What the hell?"

The others catch up behind me. All of us stand there, in shock as the car we came in drives off. Juliet is nowhere to be seen. A cloud of dust and snow trail behind her.

"Who left the damn keys in the car?" I scream.

Everyone looks at each other in astonishment. I thought I could trust her. What could literally drive her away from me? I regret not asking more questions after I found her almost dead. I knew she was hiding something. I felt her heart race as she lied right to my face, and I was stupid enough to leave her alone. I should have kept her by my side

"Where is she going?" Arthur asks.

I remember our conversation when she woke up from astral projecting. I tell them about what Juliet found while astral projecting.

"Saint Joan's convent," I say as I watch the dusty snow trail. "She was trying to find Lilith.

I feel an emptiness in my chest. I know my heart hasn't been beating for years now, but ever since Juliet came into my life, I've felt a lump in my chest I could never quite figure out. She has given my heart a second chance at life. She makes me feel like I am truly alive and not an immortal.

"Where is the convent located?" I ask.

"Somewhere hidden in the forests of Massachusetts." Victoria says, with her phone out. "It was built in the nineteen hundreds and has been abandoned ever since. It makes sense that Lilith would be hiding there, it is completely hidden. "

Massachusetts out of all the places she could have been going. Our home state, and they are hiding right under our noses. I don't know if she will be strong enough to handle herself. I didn't want to tell her, but she doesn't exactly know how to effectively use her magic. She is always finding herself in life-threatening situations. This is basically a death sentence for her.

"Then we are going,"

"Are you out of your mind?" Arthur pins me to the wall. "You are always trying to save this girl. Clearly she doesn't want to be saved."

A surge of anger sweeps over me. I know he has never liked Juliet from the start. He even went as far as locking her in the basement and starving her, just so she could be out of his way, so he wouldn't have to bother with her. He only cares about people if they have even the slightest use to him. My hands tremble as Arthur holds me against the wall. I turn on him and pin him against the wall the way he had me. Bristol and Allister stand by, ready to defend their father.

"Back up. I will tear him into a thousand pieces," I growl.

"You don't know what you are doing," Bristol pleads.

"I know exactly what I am doing." I push harder on Arthur's neck. "Arthur is selfish. He doesn't care about anyone but himself."

I release Arthur from my grip. He rubs his neck. Even though I expect him to lash out at me, he keeps his cool. Bristol comes to Arthur's side, checking if he's okay.

"That girl is trouble. She will never fix this," Arthur says.

"How would we even get there? We have no means of transportation." Bristol adds. "We can't just run on the side of the highway."

An older vampire creeps out of the double doors behind us. It's obvious that he was listening to us through the door. None of these feral vampires have any sense of privacy when it comes to others' conversations.

"Sorry to interrupt," he clasps his hands together. "We have an older automobile in the back we have not used for ages. It still starts. Only if you would feel comfortable with its return. It belonged to our oldest vampire, who recently passed."

I follow the vampire to the back of the house. His small strides leave me impatient. He dangles the keys in his hands like bells on Christmas day. The door creaks open on rusty hinges, paints flakes off into the snow. Dust covers the dashboard, and the leather is cold and rough and it almost cracks from years of inactivity.. It takes a few turns to start. The exhaust leaks a black mist.

"Are you sure this is safe?" Arthur asks.

"Most definitely," the vampire steps away from the car. "It shall get you to your destination."

Bristol waits outside the car while the rest of us are inside and buckled. Arthur gives Bristol an unsatisfying look.

"Child, get in the car!" he shouts.

A grimace crosses Bristol's lips. She cocks her knee to the side and rolls her eyes. She shakes her head ever so slightly, as if not to set off Arthur. Her small movements prove she is sacred to say something.

"Bristol. You foolish child, get in the car." Arthur's eyes turn black.

"I don't want this. We are always going after Juliet and saving her. Everything is about her. What about me? If I am about to die, I don't want to spend my time running after a girl who clearly doesn't care about us."

There's a sense of uneasiness in Bristol's voice. But her feelings are true and heartfelt. She has lived her entire life doing whatever she wants to do because she has no responsibilities. Being a vampire has its perks. Bristol never has to worry about living up to beauty standards or worry about finishing high school. Then, Juliet comes into her life and turns everything upside down. Bristol has every reason to defy her father.

"Not with this again," Arthur huffs.

"She doesn't want to come. Let her stay," I interrupt.

"You just got cross with me over wanting to stay here, did you not?"

"You have treated Juliet like complete shit ever since her arrival. You owe it to her this time. Bristol never once turned away from Juliet. That is all you did."

Arthur's lips twitch, and his eyebrows crease with revulsion. He has lost this fight, and can no longer control Bristol. Arthur waves his hand as he rolls up the window.

"Let us know if she comes back, please."

Bristol nods her head.

Allister sits beside me, and Arthur and Victoria rest in the backseat. Victoria clutches her bag to her chest. Arthur stares at the seat in front of him, and Allister fidgets in his seat. Our minds are drifting in separate directions, all focused on something different, but one thing we all have in common is if we can't find Juliet, we will cease to exist. All of this hard work would have been done for nothing. No one is safe.

Chapter Fifteen

Before I came back to school, Edith had taught me to drive. I had my learner's permit and everything. I usually practiced in the church parking lot, and occasionally drove down the street to the gas station. It never failed that Edith would hold onto what I call the "oh shit" handle. The handle right above the seats nearest to the window. Her fingers would turn white from holding on to it so tight.

Every turn I would make, she would gasp. Sometimes I would run over the curb and she would just stare at me and scold me about it once we made it back to the house.

Even after the brief lessons, I've managed to make it this far without breaking one traffic law. Come to think of it, I haven't seen a lot of state troopers in the area. I must be doing something right if I haven't wrecked the car yet. *Knock on wood.*

Magic has its perks. I used to get so lost in Cambridge. I couldn't tell north from south, or left to right. I was completely clueless about navigation. It's not something I am skilled at. Luckily, before returning to school, I had come across a spell that would help me navigate to where I needed to go. A simple chant and I follow the stars.

I've been thinking of Edith for the past few days. Her face won't leave my head. I've gone back and forth with the idea of seeing her before this all blows up in my face. It's a risky move, But I have to see her again before my possible death. I want to hug her and apologize to her face for how poorly I have treated her. She deserves my deepest apologies.

I know I have no house to go back to. All that's left is debris. I know one palace that Edith will be, by no doubt. The church. I have to get there.

After hours of driving, and only stopping a few times for gas, I have finally made it into town. I put my hood up to avoid prying eyes. No one can know I'm here. It would raise too many questions. I can't risk anyone from the church seeing me. Word would spread all around town that the pyromaniac is back. I can't do that to myself and I certainly can't do that to Edith. I've caused her enough pain already.

I enter the church's parking lot. It's empty, except for Edith's old vintage car. I'm relieved to be the only one here. I don't want anyone else to see me. And I certainly don't know what Edith may have told anyone. She could have told them I died in the house fire. She probably thought I would never return to Cambridge.

I go through the double doors. I'm greeted by a statue of Jesus and his disciples. The soft sounds of contemporary christian music fill the air. I don't know if I should call out her name or meet her without a word. I don't want to scare her, but either way she will be shocked, and I have to be prepared for that.

I enter the worship hall dancing on my tiptoes, careful not to alarm her. Ahead of me is Edith, facing the altar with her hands resting in her lap. I close the doors behind me and she jumps at the click of the door. She turns to me, and all the color drains from her face. Her mouth drops.

"Aunt Edith."

"Juliet, is that really you?" She runs to me with open arms. "Are you really here?"

I nod my head as she pulls me into her chest. The warmth of her body engulfs me, and the scent of vanilla candles fills me with familiarity and comfort. I have never felt more at home than I am now. I have waited for this moment for ages. This feels so right. There are no words to describe how much she means to me in her embrace. At this moment, I realize *she* is my mother. She is the mother I have needed all along.

"Yes, I am here." I sob, as tears drench her knitted sweater.

"Where have you been?"

"All over the place, actually." I laugh, trying to mask my uneasiness.

She ushers me inside and sits me on the bench, and lays a blanket on top of my legs. She disappears into the kitchen and returns with a cup of hot tea.

"Please tell me everything," She begs.

"I wish I could," I sigh. "There's been a lot going on. I've almost died, twice."

She grabs my hand lovingly. Her eyes swell with more tears.

"Dear child, what has Samael put you through?"

His name spoken out loud from my christian aunt sends chills down my spine. I've always heard her call him Satan, and never by his proper name. She must have known more than I expected her to.

"Listen, I don't have much time," I turn to her and hold her hands in mine. "I am on my way to a place that ensures my death."

It's not easy to tell the truth, but she has to hear it. This may be the last time I ever see her or this beautiful church. I can't leave this world without making amends with her. I have resented her for years, and only now have I realized she was only trying to protect me. She may have gone about it the most awful way possible. But maybe, if she thought to just keep her emotions hidden, then my death would be easier to cope with.

She squeezes my hands tighter.

"The angels have spoken to me, Juliet. Never in direct messages, but they have alerted me to what is coming. I trust you will do the right thing."

Tears fall from her face and onto her skirt. I can't hold in my sadness anymore. I let my emotions flow out freely. There's an empty pit in my stomach that won't go away. Thoughts eat at me, questions consume me. I know I don't have time to indulge in answers. But if I don't know this now, then dying will never be worth it.

"Did you ever meet my father?" I ask.

She smiles as she pats her face with her handkerchief.

"I did, but only for a short time. I only met him when Esther announced their engagement."

Esther and my father planned to marry. The thought almost revolts me. I'm still trying to piece together how my father could love such an evil woman. Her thoughts and actions proved her to be unfit as a mother, and unloving enough to be a wife. Unless she loved him so much, she couldn't bear the thought of living a life without him. It's still so wrong of her to willingly sacrifice me when I had no say. She still used me. I will forever despise her for that.

"He was the complete opposite of Esther."

It warms my heart to know that Aunt Edith had the pleasure in meeting my father. She never understood his love for my mother, and maybe he wanted to change her ways. Esther was filled with a magic that should have repulsed my father, but somehow he saw something inside her.

I feel a sense of comfort in calling my mother by her name. Edith didn't so much as flinch when she heard the name escape my mouth. It seems the both of us have come to the conclusion that Esther is no longer part of this family, and will never be addressed as my mother. She is known only as a person who held me in her womb. She is nothing in my eyes.

The conversation went better than I expected. I gave myself anxiety just for nothing. I can tell she is truly proud of me. Although she wishes I'd never left her side, she knows I'm nothing like my mother, and I'm becoming more like my father every day.

Leaving Edith is nothing more than sincere and full of tears. She begs me to stay, but she understands my need to leave and save the others I care about. I try to remember her touch, the way her skin feels on mine, and the warmth of her chest. I try so hard to keep those memories embedded in my head.

***

It's late by the time I am back in Massachusetts. I still can't believe Samael and Lilith had been hiding there all along, and never made themselves known. I wish we had known of their location before we traveled to Maine. I could have found a solution much sooner, and more lives could have been spared. That's if I could even stop Lilith.

I drive through a strange town I'm not familiar with. I've only traveled so far while in Massachusetts, so this twin is new to me. A plethora of shops line the street, all ranging from gift shops to clothing shops, metaphysical and occult shops. I know Massachusetts holds people of many backgrounds. People of all practices live here, and someone has to know what is going on in the immortal world.

Witchcraft wasn't always confined to just Salem. In fact, there was little to no witchcraft there at all during the Salem Witch Trials. The witches were too clever to be found. They could never expose themselves in such a town that was ridden with religious folk. Even the more experienced witches couldn't risk being near Salem during the time of the hangings.

Most of the so-called witches were ordinary people. They were only called witches for their unorthodox way of life. No one accepted people who lived differently. That's kind of how I feel. I'm not an evil person, I just chose to live differently than others.

I walk for what seems like ages. I pass by many witch shops, but always get the wrong vibe from each one. Some shops are strictly tarot card businesses, others sell crystals and ouija boards. I walk past an occult bookstore, and through the window, three books are displayed, a religious journal on both sides, and in the middle stands an intricate Bible.

The store's lights are dimly lit. I enter, as it might be my last hope. The bell loudly rings as the tip of the door touches the bell. I hear no sound from the outside. The silence is eerie.

"Hello, welcome!"

A tall, older, and well-dressed woman comes around the corner of the office. Her long skirt flows behind her, and her bracelets jingle against each other. Her long grey hair is neatly tied into a braid that swoops down her back. Wrinkles line her face, revealing the many years of living.

"What can I help you find?" She asks kindly.

I look around the shelves. Every book has its own place, and everything is neatly sorted into different genres. There are Bibles of all editions, big and small, plain and colorful. I've never seen so many Bibles in one place besides the church where Edith and I attend. It makes me wonder if she ever knew this place existed. She'd have too much fun here.

"I am just looking," I run my fingers across the hardback books. "What wonderful store you have."

The woman laughs. She continues to eye me. She senses that I'm completely out of my comfort zone.

"Thankyou, has been in the family for quite some time."

I stop at a shelf that is lined with books about angels, the different hierarchies of the angels, and where they are talked about in the Bible.

"Actually, I need directions as well. Do you know where St. Joan's Convent is?"

She drops her arms from her chest.

"Dear, why would you want to go there? It's been abandoned for ages now."

"Curiosity," I mumble.

I continue to walk around the aisle while she watches me closely. I feel the roughness of the pentagram on my arm and it begins to itch. She watches me rustle with my shirt.

"Oh, dear, you are bleeding."

I hurry to look at my shirt and a small drop of blood seeps through. I knew I should have wrapped it with something before I left.

"Oh, it's nothing, just a scratch." I hold my opposite hand over the scar to apply pressure to it. The pressure doesn't help, and the blood seeps more into the shirt. You can now see the outline of the entire pentagram.

The woman's eyes stay locked on my mark.

"Are you the witch?" she whispers.

I stare at her, making sure I heard her correctly.

"What do you mean, the witch?"

She comes closer to me and rubs her eyes to get a clearer view of my face.

"You're the daughter of Esther Arden, aren't you?"

To hear her name come from a stranger sets me on edge. I hate being associated with such an evil woman. I don't want to be referred to as her daughter or any family title. Did this woman know of her evil and what she did to me? Surely she does. Otherwise, she wouldn't have asked me if I was Esther's daughter. It even baffles me more that a woman running a christian store would know who Esther is.

"Yes. I am."

The minute I answer, her hands go up in the air. Not in fear, but in joy. The woman returns to the register and searches for something on the shelves beneath her. She pulls out a book with a brochure sticking out of it. The dust floats into their air around us, causing me to choke.

She hands me the brochure. "This is a map of the surrounding area. St Joan's Convent is just outside the city, tucked away behind trees."

I observe the map. The black and red lines intimidate me as they intertwine together.

"I take it you need little protection?" Our eyes lock. "Your father was an angel."

I stare at her, wondering how she knew such information. I thought only the people close to me knew about my family history. I wondered how many people actually knew my mother and father.

"How did you know?"

"Everyone knows the story of how you were brought up. Satan wanted you from the very beginning. All immortals know everything. News travels."

I lower my head. A heaviness in my stomach leaves me nauseous. The lump in my throat makes it harder to breathe. I feel so much guilt for causing so much harm and death to innocent people. My mother has given me this curse to bear, and she's not even here, so I can kill her for it.

"I have never met my father nor am I able to make contact." I lower my head.

"Take this," She hands me a rosary. "Whatever you are up against, they will be expecting you to use their magic. Use the gifts your father has passed down to you."

The black and grey beading lined all the way to the pointed cross. Dust lingers on the rosary. Who knows how long the rosary was sitting in a box behind her desk. Such a beautiful thing to own. I do feel a connection to it, though. I feel closer to my father, whom I have never met.

"I can't take this." I hold out the rosary.

"Yes, Juliet you can."

I don't remember giving her my name, but she said people all over knew my name and knew what I did. I can't thank her enough for her kind gestures and her positivity. Her life was on the line too, and when this was all over, I had to come back to thank her personally.

I navigate through the late night stragglers. Driving out of the street of a small town wasn't easy. I'm stalled for about five minutes, all because of a drunken man passing out in the middle of the road. His friend finds him and drags him to the gutter, giving me a thumbs up.

As I get further away from the city, I continue to eye the rosary hanging in the rearview mirror. I almost feel as if it was speaking directly to me. I find comfort in its existence. Scenes flash through my mind of what I think my father would have looked like. I imagine growing up with him around. He'd teach me how to ride a bike, get me through my first break up, and walk me down the aisle. These are all dreams and all without my demon of a mother.

I continue to fantasize about what my life would have been like if my father hadn't died. I almost miss my turn, and one street light snaps me out of my trance right before I turn. The road is dark and dusty, bordered by large trees that make the sky look darker than it is. I feel trapped, almost as if I'm driving to my own funeral.

I see the convent ahead. At the gates, I see one poorly lit torch. I'm surprised they even lit a torch. Surely they wouldn't want just anyone stumbling too far and finding this place. Or maybe that's exactly what they want. Somehow, they have to know that I'd be coming to them.

I never constructed a plan for when I arrived. I can't just walk into the building, walk up to Lilith, and act like best friends. Demons can be standing to guard at the gates. I have no protection other than the rosary the eccentric woman gave me, but it's enough to ensure my safety. I have no knowledge of banishing a demon. I have no idea how to tap into my angel gifts, if I have any. Right now, I have to accept my death.

I have a strange urge to pray. I had only prayed a few times in my life, most of when I was only five years old, when Edith began to preach to me. I don't know what to say. I almost need to write a speech just to pray to God. I knew how to pray. I just don't think it would be genuine.

I approach the side of the convent that I didn't travel to in the astral state. The iron gates tower feet over me. They peer down at me with unwelcoming eyes of steel. I pull the gate with one hand and hold onto the rosary with another. The gate is unlocked. I suddenly feel I should not have come alone. Lilith and Samael knew I'd be here. How stupid can I possibly be?

"Oh, Juliet."

The wind brushes past my ear, and a whisper runs down my ear canal. Chills race up my spine and the back of my head becomes warm. They know I'm here, but I can't turn back now. I've come too far to back down now.

"Juliet, come." The voice floats through the air.

Before I can think, my legs are driving me toward the whispers. It must have been another trick of Samael's. He uses complete body control.

Through the double doors of the convent, I am greeted with two torches that line the stone walls. Two cathedral type windows let in the light of the moon. The gothic style convent is nothing holy. It feels nothing but cold and ominous. My eyes can't adjust to the darkness that sits at the end of the hallway.

"You're almost there Juliet." a laugh echoes off the walls.

I wrap my jacket around me for warmth. You'd think Satan's lair would be hot like the home he's from. No matter how hard I rub my shoulders, chills still crawl through my body.

As I turn the corner, the smell of sulfur and rotting corpses invades me. The smell isn't so pungent now, as it was when the demons came into my house, but still, it's an awful smell.

I come to the end of the hallway, greeted by a statue of Mother Mary. Her graceful hands clasp together, looking down upon me. I can only imagine seeing her grief as she watched her son be hung from a cross, shamed and completely broken, only for him to rise without a scratch on him. I have to be like her, strong and fearless.

I look above the doorway. It holds the same cross my Aunt Edith has hanging over her front door. I find comfort in the thought of her.

I push through the doors as I inhale. Hundreds of torches light up the enormous cathedral. The majority looks new, but others look as though they had been smouldering with fire after being thrown across the room. The stone titles are blackened to the point it will never come off. The evil is forever etched into this consecrated church.

Ahead of me is a big pit of fire. Screeching voices linger in the inside it; the souls of the immortals. Demons in red robes settle around the fire, close enough to burn their already incinerated flesh. They make no move to my entrance. They stand completely still in their haze, almost like gargoyles protecting their masters. Their black wings form a circle around the fire.

"Glad of you to join us, Juliet." Lilith ascends out of the pit of fire. Her skin is glowing more than it ever has before. Her hair still hangs over her shoulders and tossed around. This time, she's covered in a simple red dress that plunges a little too low on her chest. Her bare feet are singed from the coals of the fire.

Lilith glides to her lover in the corner. Samael looks displeased with my presence, but entertains Lilith to the fullest.

"Look, my love, It's Juliet." She kisses Samael on the cheek. "The one who brought me back to you."

Her wicked voice vibrates in her throat, almost animal-like. She smiles from ear to ear, and her pearly white teeth show through. I can tell her mental state is completely obliterated. She has almost a Harley Quinn personality; funny and terrifying to witness. Samael must have been so proud of what he has. I guess the more power she draws from the immortals, the more her brain loses its grip on reality.

The high ceiling goes up for many feet. Its intricate design is ages old. The architecture is classical. The paintings tell a story of Jesus's birth and ascension to heaven. The paint is chipping around the edges, leaving a medieval feel to it.

"I am here to make a deal with you."

CHAPTER SIXTEEN

Lilith circles around the pit of fire. I wish she wouldn't look at me with those demonic eyes. I fear if I looked into them for too long, she might possess my soul.

"You have helped us enough, witch," She hisses.

"You will want to hear this."

Last minute I devise another plan; a plan I will forever regret, and Keelan will never forgive me for. My throat strains to speak.

"Kill me, take my witch and angelic powers, and leave the rest of the immortals alone." I slide to Lilith. "I would be the perfect sacrifice."

Lilith focuses on Samael with curious eyes.

"We have more guests." Lilith smiles.

The door behind me swings open, and a breeze travels over me. The fire dances with the air. Demons with red robes pan into view, each of them holding hostages to their rotting bodies. Familiar faces enter the room. Keelan, Allister, Arthur and Victoria. Bristol is nowhere to be found.

"What are you doing?" Keelan calls.

Keelan struggles under the clutch of the demons. He doesn't show any signs of physical trauma. They must have made it here right after I did. Victoria probably did a tracking spell to see exactly how I got here.

"No, Keelan. What are you doing here?" I step closer to them, but the demon's grip tighter, almost breaking their bones. They cry out in pain.

"Saving you," Keelan pulls away, but the demon's claws dig into him further. "You shouldn't have come alone, or at all."

Lilith steps in between Keelan and I. She circles around Keelan with a smile plastered on her face. I can see she's intrigued by his return. I don't want a repeat of past events. I don't want to see the vile things she could do to lure men in.

"Juliet, will you tell your boyfriend what you really came here for?" Lilith giggles.

Tears block my vision. I wipe them away with my sleeve. I look down at the dried blood on my shirt. The bleeding is triggered by the presence of evil.

"Why don't you tell them all how you planned to sacrifice yourself to save all the immortal kind?"

Keelan's eyes turn black, the skin around his eyes fade red, and tears stream down his face. He rolls his hands into a fist. This is what I had tried to prevent from happening. I planned to sacrifice myself to save him and all the immortals. My intentions won't go as I planned, especially with Keelan now in the picture.

"That's not true." Keelan's voice cracks. "Juliet, tell me that isn't true."

His voice breaks my heart more than anything. He shouldn't be here. This is not supposed to happen. He is making this harder than it should be. I hate him for always trying to stop me. I hate how he can't let me be independent, even if this does involve him. I wish he could push past his love for me and see that I am trying to keep him alive.

"It's the only way to save you, Keelan." My breath becomes uncontrollable. My cries vibrate off the walls.

"So you are just going to give yourself up and die, without saying goodbye?"

"Saying goodbye would have made this harder to do. Why can't you understand that?"

I release my grip on the rosary and realize it's cutting off my circulation. My hand is white and numb. I tuck the rosary into my back pocket discreetly. There really is no use for it now. A piece of jewelry can't save me. I did have hope for it, though.

Arthur, Allister and Victoria stand still, as they are no longer struggling to escape the hold of the demons. They are in too much shock to say anything. The muddled looks on their faces scream in agony, full of sadness. I've created a memory none will forget.

Samael steps into view from the corner. He tightens his wrist watch. He wears a neatly ironed, black button-up shirt. I much rather prefer him in this appearance. It's much easier to look at him than his red evil eyes. Splattered blood peeks out of his collar. He is the king of hell and he can't bother to clean himself up.

"Listen," Samael speaks. "This truly breaks my heart."

Samael speaks lies through his demonic teeth. Fallen angels don't have the capacity to feel emotion. Everything he says he feels is a blatant lie, and anything he feels for Lilith is only infatuation. There is no room for love in his evil heart; if he even had one.

I sit on the pew in front of the fire, facing away from Keelan and the others. I don't want to look at Keelan. I don't want to see the heartbreak smeared across his face. I wish he could understand what I am doing, not only for him, but for all the immortal kind. I am trying to undo what I have done. What Esther has done.

"Back to business," Lilith jumps. "My love, do you think she would be the perfect sacrifice?"

Samael grins and puts his arm around Lilith. She twirls her hair in her fingers, licking her lips so slightly, you can see the leftover blood in the cracks of her teeth.

Samael stands in front of me and kneels to my level. His hot breath grazes over my ear. He rips off the sleeve of my shirt and observes the sigil embedded into my arm. His psyche seems off, like he isn't all the way there, like he has lost part of himself. He tilts his head to my arm and brings mouth to my arm and licks the wound from top to bottom. I freeze, and my heart pumps out of my chest. This man is absolutely mad.

"She has a lot of power, Lilith," He wipes his mouth. "She would be perfect for what we have planned. Her blood tastes amazing too."

Keelan struggles and frees himself from the demon's hold. He dashes down the aisles. But before he can get close to me, Samael raises his hand and Keelan freezes in the air, in a paralyzed state. Keelan is so blinded by love he risks his own life.

"This is what love does," Samael laughs. "Love is a weakness. Love makes people make stupid decisions."

"I have an idea better than sacrificing yourself." Lilith comes to me.

I can finally see through her raging green eyes, full of hunger and hate. I see the lust on her lips. She craves power and acceptance over Samael. I can see right through her uneasiness. Her physical body cannot handle the mentality she faces.

"How about you watch all of your friends die a slow, painful death, and then we kill you?" Her red lips spread to an unstable grin, almost clown-like. The way her face stretches is unreal.

She isn't going to take my offer. She would rather see her immortal children die than accept the sacrifice of one powerful witch. Nothing I say or do will change her mind. She is fixed on seeing her kind suffer, all for the glory of Samael.

"Take them."

The demons take Keelan and the others out of the sanctuary. Victoria's screams reverberate off the walls. Samael grabs me by my neck and drags me in the same direction as the others. The cold stone cuts into my skin through my pants. I have no time to scream in pain, but imagine the horror of watching my friends die. I'll soon have the same experience as Esther. Nothing I do now will help. No spell or incantation will stop this. *I have failed.*

We enter a long corridor in complete darkness. I trip over rocks and my own feet. Samael's hot hands are still secured onto the back of my neck, causing bruising to happen quickly. His body presses against mine and I want nothing more to release all my power into him, but I know I'd fail miserably.

"Here, front-row seat." Samael laughs.

Samael throws me to the cold ground. The only light comes from the broken window above me. Keelan and the others face me across the hall in a different cell. Their fallen faces don't look up. They sit defeated and slowly accept their death sentence.

I can't understand why a convent would have cells like this. I can't picture a nun being down here, secluded from the rest of her sisters. Is this the kind of punishment nuns faced when they went against God?

"I am genuinely sorry for the pain I have caused," I mumble. "If I would have never gone home the night of the dance, we wouldn't be here."

Keelan looks up to me, for he remembered the night, too. Vividly, I remember being so disturbed at the sight of Keelan, thinking he was dead for all this time. I can still feel his icy hand on my skin for the first time in months since the accident. He can hear my thoughts as I reminisce. I want him to remember. It may be the last thing he sees before leaving this world forever.

"Don't be sorry." Keelan sighs. "If I would have just warned you sooner. If I hadn't faked my death, then maybe we could have avoided all of this. We could have been together sooner. I should have done more to protect you. Instead, I was selfish, terrified at the idea I would die at the hands of the Elder's. I thought I was doing good by respecting their orders."

That is right. He was being selfish, but I can't stay mad at him for that. He was only looking out for himself and the others. How could he let a witch like me come into his life and dismantle it from the inside out?

My brain clicks. I realize Bristol isn't present. She must have stayed behind at the vampire coven in Maine. I can't imagine the heartbreak she must be feeling right now. She will never have the chance to say goodbye to her family. Bristol will die alone with people who don't know her like we do. There had to be a bigger reason she stayed behind. Something tells me it's because of me.

As I sit there, the moon beaming down on me. I think of everything that has happened in my life. From my childhood all the way to now, almost as if my life is flashing before my eyes, like I am on the brink of death. Now that I think about it, I should have died months ago. I should have died in the fire.

I would do anything right now to be with Regina and Edith. I crave the warmth and familiarity of her presence. My heart drops to my stomach at the thought of Regina never knowing of my fate. She could be in her bedroom right now, crying and conjuring thoughts of where I could be. Same goes for Brody. We left on very bad terms, but all the words we exchanged were spoken out of anger and sorrow. I'd never be able to apologize for reacting the way I did.

I need my Aunt Edith's wise words. She would know what to do at this moment. Coming from a family of both witches and angels, she must have known how to handle this. I can't comprehend the knowledge she must have known from all the years in the church. She knew the ins and outs of the Bible. Reading it from top to bottom, she analyzed it thoroughly, and repeated the process. She deconstructed each verse of the Bible to find it's true meaning. She's a very devoted woman, and I look up to her for that.

The rosary twists in my pocket, leaving an uncomfortable lump as I sit on the hard stone. I unravel its beauty, admiring the intricate beads and creativity. In the center of the cross, a jewel shines the brightest. A sparkle takes me by surprise, the one similar to when Victoria and I touched for the first time. It's as if the rosary is speaking to me.

I get on my knees, and the rosary dangles between my hands. I remember how to pray with a rosary just from watching Edith do it for years.

"What are you doing?" Keelan asks.

"She is praying," Victoria responds.

"She is a witch, she can't—"

"She is part angel. She knows what she is doing."

I tune out their whispers. I mumble through the lord's prayer, each time speaking faster and louder. I hear shuffling in front of me. Keelan and the others are uncomfortable with my praying. I continue on in hopes to connect with my father. He had to have answers.

"Father, I ask you to come forth in this time of uncertainty.Father please, I need you, I need your wisdom." I squeeze the rosary. "Michael, I call on you."

Chapter Seventeen

The moon light becomes brighter, igniting the entire cell. Keelan and the others crouch in the corner, shielding their eyes. The monotone sound of trumpets ring through the room. It's a beautiful and peaceful sound, yet frightening.

The moon's light transforms into a beam of light, so bright I can barely stand to look at it. The temperature changes around me and I feel a calmness rush over me. I've never felt so at peace and so safe.

Particles of light shimmer before me. Colors of gold and silver sprinkle on the ground in front of me. As I look up from the rosary, the light forms into a silhouette of a man. His feet come into view, slowly sliding up his body and the figure becomes clearer.

The light dims, and a tall man stands before me. I expected him to be dressed in a white robe topped with a golden halo and enormous white wings clinging to his back. That is what the angels are depicted as in the paintings. He appears more normal than ever; a plain t white t-shirt and denim pants.

"Are you Michael?" I whisper. I cling to the rosary.

"Yes, Juliet." He holds his hands out in a welcoming way. "It is so great to finally meet you, daughter."

We embrace without hesitation. Love overwhelms me. I never knew I could feel this emotion so heavily. The sensation washes over me like I had known him my entire life, and maybe he has been watching me for the eighteen years I have been alive. I knew he was always there beside me, through every good and bad decision.

"It's really you," I cry.

I breathe in his scent, and I'm taken back to a clean forest filled with fresh cedar and cherries. Visions pass through my mind of what could have been. They feel like memories, but it's more like a reality that could have been. I almost forget where I am and what is going on.

He breaks our embrace and helps me to my feet. Keelan stands by with his hands wrapped around the bars that separate us. He, too, is in awe of Michael's theatrical entrance.

"I'm so glad you finally called for me. I have been waiting so long."

"I just prayed, I didn't know this would happen."

"You had faith, Juliet, that is all that matters," He smiles.

If I had known about him when I was younger, I would have called him much earlier than this, not when I'm about to die. It seems so easy to do. I regret not asking more questions about him. I could have talked to him regularly. We could have formed a relationship in some way. My demise for the church and Edith had blinded me to all the powers I possessed.

I want to hug him again, to really feel his presence. Looking away from him is hard. His beauty is like nothing I have ever seen before.

"I am sure you know what's going on," I scratch my head. " I don't know what to do."

"Yes, you do. You have your mother's gifts."

I cringe when he speaks of my mother. I never thought he would mention her, considering she's a witch, and he's an angel. The two just don't mix. It's an abomination in the eyes of the Lord. She may have been powerful enough to summon the Devil, but I don't want to be compared to her, not in the slightest.

I don't want to be like her in any way. I used to when I was little, but I have learned so much about her in the past few days that just don't sit right with me. It goes everything against my morals. I don't even want to have kids now that I know the truth about her. I never want the thought to touch my mind, and to coerce me into sacrificing an innocent child. Acts from the past will repeat themselves, only if we don't correct them in the present. Every decision she made, I will do the opposite. That is if I live to see the sun rise.

"I'm not powerful enough," I breathe.

"Yes, you are. You are on two sides of the spectrum, good and, well you know."

He means evil. I am both good and evil. I was finally at peace with knowing my mother was an evil woman, and he thought so, too. She never cared about me, and she was selfish in her ways. I don't regret leaving her the way I did. I still don't see how my father could have fallen in love with her. I didn't see how they could have made me.

Michael looks at Keelan and the others cowering in the corner, and they lock eyes. It's as if all sound has disappeared from the Earth. Here comes the father and boyfriend talk I have been dreading.

Michael walks to Keelan. They both continue to keep eyes on each other, both waiting for the other to give it up.

"Thank you," Michael says.

Keelan cocks his head.

"Thank you, for protecting my daughter when I couldn't," Michael lowers his eyes. "I wish I could do more to show you how much I appreciate all your sacrifices. I know our species clash, but you have given a life to Juliet. I wish I could have given her."

Keelan drops his hands off the bars. His mind is spinning with questions. I don't think he was expecting to have this type of conversation.

"I'm so sorry it has come to this," Keelan cries. "I wish I could have done more. I feel like I have failed her."

Michael rests his hand on Keelan's. Keelan becomes uncomfortable with the holiness of Michael.

"She is still alive. You could have never stopped this from happening. Don't beat yourself up about it. You may be a bloodsucker, but you are filled with love and kindness."

Tears flood my eyes. I thought I'd never hear something like that in my lifetime. It took me this long to realize that Keelan is the one for me, the one I want to spend the rest of my life with, even if I am to die minutes from now.

Michael returns to my side.

"Is there any way to help us?" I ask.

Michael pinches the bridge of his nose. That is all he has to do before I realize there is nothing he can do. *Don't say it. Don't say it.*

"No," He breathes. "I do not have the skills as the Powers do. I am here only for words of encouragement. And to meet my only daughter."

I don't regret calling him forth. In fact, I am relieved I did, because I may never have another chance before my death. I want him to stay longer. We have eighteen years to make up for in only a short time, but it's near impossible. I need my father in my life, no matter who says otherwise.

Tears stream down my face. The numbness travels along my skin. There is nothing to do other than cherish these last moments with the ones I love the most.

"Although you are part of me, I am not sure where you will go when we part ways. I love you, Juliet and please don't ever forget that."

Michael turns to Victoria, who stands crouched in the corner, with her arms crossing her body.

"I trust you will take good care of her, won't you, Victoria?"

He calls her by her name. If he had ever met her while he was still alive, he would have said something from the start. But maybe he knew that because he's an angel. He knows we share magic. It's only right if witches stick together.

Victoria nods her head.

The moon beams down into a bright light again. The light and tears blind me for a moment. He stands in the middle of the beam and he fades into particles of light. I catch a glance at him before he disappears. His smile never leaves, and I am left with the feeling of peace.

"Well, that was very unhelpful if I may add," Allister interrupts.

Keelan whips around to Allister and pins him against the wall. Allister's eyes are empty, yet a wicked smile spreads across his face.

"Shut up. We are all in the same situation. She met her father for the first time and you have the audacity to say such a thing? If we weren't in this situation right now, I would not hesitate to snap your neck, even if Bristol was here."

Allister falls to the ground and chuckles to himself. He is on the brink of insanity. We all are. Samael's perfect plan is coming into play and destroying all of our lives in the blink of an eye. Allister no longer cares if he lives or dies. He has given up.

Arthur grunts from the corner of the room. Keelan and Allister run to his side.

"What is wrong, father?"

Allister reaches to his forehead. Victoria rushes to his side with worried eyes. Her gentle cries ring through the cell.

"He is feverish," Allister mutteres. "He will not be alive much longer."

This is what Lilith meant when she said we would watch each other die. We didn't have time on our side anymore. Arthur is dying, and I have no spell to reverse the effects, neither does Victoria. I underestimated Lilith's power.

Victoria and I exchange looks of grief. She can feel the emptiness that I feel. I hear her thoughts inside my head. We have never communicated this way before. It startles me, but I connect with her. We listen to each other's voices ring through our minds.

Break through the bars.

Set this place on fire.

Use their own power against them.

Victoria and I face each other on each side of the bars that separate us. We grip onto the bars and firmly stand our ground. Victoria mumbles a spell to break the barriers. And I chant the

Lord's prayer. The bars rattle against the rust. The bars creak under the power of a witch and an angel.

The bars, one by one, unhinge from the holes in the ground. The metal rods sound against the hard floor and an opening emerges for us to unite. Keelan pushes through Victoria and embraces me with arms so strong. His body is still cold, so I know he is still untouched by Lilith, but will soon fall victim to her death games.

"I'm so sorry," I cry. "I am sorry I left you. I thought I was doing the right thing.

Keelan kisses me passionately.

"Do not apologize. I know why you did it," He brushed the hair behind my ear. "But I couldn't bear the thought of finding you dead."

Victoria goes around the cell to find any protection spells that keep us in here. She raises her hand to the stone walls to feel the energy inside it. Her hands tremble as she mutters an incantation.

"Arthur is too weak," Keelan sighs. "Soon he will be gone."

Keelan's voice cracks, almost as if he's trying to stop himself from crying. This is all becoming too real for us to measure.

"I will stay with him," Allister adds. "I cannot let my father die alone."

"And what of Bristol? You could have fought harder for her to come with," I cry.

Victoria spins to Arthur, who is now laying on his side. His shallow breaths come slowly and sweat drips down his face. The magic that keeps him alive is diminishing. All he has is the power of love in his heart.

Victoria caresses Arthur's face. He grabs her hand gently.

"You must go. I am no longer of any service to any of you."

"This just isn't fair," Victoria mumbles. She cries into Arthur's neck.

"We have to go now," Keelan demands.

Keelan leads us out of the long hallway that we came through earlier. She wipes her tears away from her face as she is the last to leave. I hear her sobs as we jog down the hallway. She tries to muffle her cris, but the stone walls aren't soundproof.

Keelan stops at a corner that's ignited by a dimly lit torch. He presses his back to the wall, concealing himself in the shadows. Victoria and I mimic his actions. Keelan peaks around the corner and swiftly retreats. He closes his eyes, and takes a breath.

"The demons," He whispers. "At least ten of them. But I can't see if Samael or Lilith is in the room."

I look at Victoria, who has kept her eyes down the entire time. Her emotions are overtaking her and blocking her from the present. She has other things on her mind. She wants to be with Arthur. It kills me to see her so distraught. But now is not the time to let emotions consume us. Our minds have to be in this if we are going to come out alive.

"There is no way to get to the sanctuary without going through this corridor. We won't make it to the sanctuary in one piece."

"Juliet. I'm so glad to have met you," Victoria says.

Keelan and I look at her with confused eyes.

"Tell Edith, I love her."

"What are you talking about? How do you know Edith?" My eyes search her. My heart picks up speed.

"The spark. When we first met. It happens when two witches of the same bloodline touch." She uses her sleeve to wipe her face, smearing her mascara. "It wasn't long after that, I discovered who you are. You are my niece."

"Impossible. Edith would have told me about you."

"No, she wouldn't have. I left the family at such a young age. Arthur is the man I left the family for." She takes my hand in hers. "Edith and Esther are my younger sisters."

I rest against the wall behind me. My brain can't process the information fast enough to form a response.

"That's why my father said what he said, about protecting me. He knows who you are."

I should feel hatred towards Victoria. I should despise her for keeping something like this from me. Why would she choose now to tell me? The moment we met, she had to know who I was. My last name should have given it away. She kept this huge secret from me this entire time. *I can't believe this is happening.*

I catch a glimpse of Victoria's green eyes before she darts into the corridor full of demons. She leaves too fast. I couldn't grab onto her fast enough without being seen.

Her monotone voice rings in the hallway. I pounced at her, but fell to the ground. She's gone. Keelan pulls me up. My knees are weak. My eyes swell with tears and my stomach feels heavy. Everything is spinning in slow motion.

"We have to go, Juliet," Keelan pulls me through the doorway.

My feet move underneath me, but it's like I'm floating on a cloud.

"I can't let her do this!" I sob.

Keelan searches for the demons, but they are nowhere to be found. Suddenly, screaming echoes off the walls of the convent. They got her. They are killing her.

"Juliet, we can mourn later. Now is not the time."

Keelan squeezes my hand as we navigate the halls of the convent. At any moment Samel could catch us at the corner, and I have to be ready to fight to the death. I'm prepared to use all of my magic to destroy him.

We round the corner to the front entrance. Keelan and I stop and stare at each other, contemplating if we should exit the convent or go inside the sanctuary, where we know where Samael and Lilith are hiding. We both know that once we step into the sanctuary, there will be no going back. The only way we'd leave is if they kill us.

"If we leave now, we can find a spot far from here and just fade into nothing."

I pull my hand away from Keelan's. I can't believe what I just heard.

"Are you serious? You want to give up that easily?"

"We are just a vampire and a witch," Keelan sighs. "We can't beat Samael or his demons. If we could, then we would have defeated him back in Stull."

"I am more than a witch. I am half angel. I can take him on. I'm not scared."

Self-deception is something I do. If I tell myself lies then maybe they'd become the truth. But I am scared. I'm so terrified. There is no way I can do this. But there has to be a fighting chance. I have to die, knowing that I tried to stop this evil. People have to know that I didn't go out without a fight.

Keelan looks out the tiny window next to the double doors.

"Do you trust me?"

Keelan nods his head.

"We will die trying."

"Die together," Keelan says.

The double doors fly off the hinges and into the air with a sway of my hand. The adrenaline pumps through me, and aids my last bit of energy to fight, and it takes away my fears. I don't think about the outcome, and I don't think about my death. All I have in mind is stopping the Lord and Lady of Darkness.

I run down the aisle, ripping the pews from the ground and throwing them into the fire of souls. The rumbling of the destruction vibrates my body.

Samael and Lilith turn to us with their wicked and fearful eyes. Never had I seen unholy beings so terrified. The creator of all things immortal, scared of a witch. She made me, and Satan gained power from me. How could they be so weak? God has spoken of them to be so cruel. I don't think that is the case anymore.

"I have been waiting for this moment," Lilith laughs.

Lilith claws at the fire, her hands engulfed in blue flames. She throws balls of fire toward Keelan and I. I wave my hand and shield myself with the holy water sitting in the stoup beside me. The hisses from the fire's expulsion are heaven to my ears.

Samael goes after Keelan. They stand apart on the two sides of the sanctuary. Keelan pulls the pews from their bolts and chucks them at Samael. But he is too fast to get hit. Keelan turns to the beautiful stained glass behind him and punches it with almost no effort. The glass shatters to the ground, and a rainbow forms in the light of the fire. Keelan throws the glass in hopes to wound Samael.

"You really think, a piece of matter will destroy me?" Samael smiles.

"It is not you I am aiming for."

Keelan yanks a pipe from the ground and throws it above Samael, hitting the chandelier that towers above him. The chair breaks loose and comes crashing down. Samael misses it by only a few inches.

Lilith treads closer to me, forgetting the power I had. Her eyes fade to black in fury. She stands feet away from me and tilts her head back, with her eyes rolling back and the whites of her eyes are noticeable. A black snake emerges from her mouth, and her throat moves with the movement of the snake. It goes on forever. The snake hisses and lunges at me with its deadly fangs.

I take control of the fire and launch it towards Lilith's beautiful face. She falls to her knees as her face is signed with the fire she made to destroy me.

"Silly girl. Don't you know? I come from the depths of hell. I take showers hotter than this."

The burnt skin falls from her face, bone showing, and face dripping in black blood. The gash leaves her unbothered.

The snake lunges at me, and I shield my face with only my arm. It wraps itself around my arm, squeezing it till I can no longer feel it. It catches my eyes and talks to me. Blood drips from my ears from the blasphemy that is spoken.

The snake twirls around me. My chest walls are being compressed into my lungs. Any moment now my ribs will cave in. I make every breath count, for I can't call for Keelan to help me.

Lilith crawls to my side, her face already healing but still badly bruised. Her orange hair falls over my face, blocking my view from Keelan and Samael.

"Stop resisting, Juliet," she traces her finger over the snake. "You have already lost. I should have killed you when I had the chance."

I avoid her eye contact and look for Keelan behind her hair. She follows my eyes to the target.

"If Samael doesn't kill him, I may keep him as my new toy."

She leans into my face. Her breath reeks of coal and sulfur. Before I can blink, Lilith is tossed to the altar and hits the ground with a bang. Her body disappears in the rubble.

Keelan comes running to my aid and rips the snake apart with his fangs. Its black blood spills into his mouth and onto the floor. The snake's limp body convulses on the floor, edging to its death. My lungs feel whole again, and they expand to the fullest. But, it's still not over.

For a moment, everything is quiet, almost peaceful. Far off, trumpets ring. A choir of beautiful harmonies vibrates off the stone walls.

Lilith collects herself and runs to her lover. Samael looks worse than ever. His chest rises and falls every second like he actually is having a hard time. Their faces are consumed with fear. They now realize that I won't back down and I won't give in. They are surprised we have lived this long.

"I'm impressed, Juliet," Samael says. "I didn't think you had the power to even get this far."

Lilith tussles with her hair and brushes the ash from her face. She has stopped healing. This is her breaking point.

"I have a proposition for you. Come to hell with Lilith and I, and I will make you the highest ranking officer in my army. You have proven yourself to be no more than capable of defeating us."

"I have not defeated you. I still see your grotesque face." I say.

I reach around to my pocket, the rosary still intact. I pull it out and secure it around my neck.

"You think that will protect you? Your soul is mine already. It is too late to play God."

I ignore his hateful words and pray under my breath.

"I call upon Seraphim, the heavenly warriors. Come shine your light on the wicked and destroy their soul."

Samael must have heard me. He grabs Lilith's arm and pulls her to the side door. I hold my hand out in a stopping motion. They freeze in their tracks.

"God will not have mercy on your damned soul."

The chandeliers shake, and the glass trickles down onto the floor. The sound of trumpets fill the sanctuary. A blinding light shines through the stained glass and an army of angels descend into the room. Their halos are made of light and fire, and their wings are whiter than I have ever seen before.

More angels barge in through the sanctuary doorway. Their faces are almost too beautiful to look at. Some carry bows and arrows, and others wield flaming swords, like the one that protected the Garden of Eden.

Blood-covered demons appear in the sanctuary. I realize they are covered in none other than Victoria's blood. Knowing that sparked the last of my energy to defeat the wickedness that is the world. Red and white clash together in the fire. Angels fly above me, merging with the demons and turning them into ash.

"This is amazing." I say.

"It sure is, daughter."

I spin around to find my father. He wields a flaming sword and a glowing halo.

"How are you here?"

"The Lord decided I needed to help you. He made me a Seraphim."

We embrace, smearing the blood on his pure white robe. His wings make it almost impossible to wrap my arms around him entirely. The feathers are so soft, like the fuzz on a peach. Everything becomes silent behind me.

I'm unaware of the actions behind me, and Michael wraps his wings around me to shield me from the incoming debris. He is too slow and a piece of wood strikes me in my shoulder. I drop to the ground and Michael stands over me, holding me.

"Juliet, no!" Keelan comes running back to Michael and I.

"I wasn't fast enough," Michael mutters.

I lay on my side as Keelan and Michael observe the wound. The adrenaline keeps me from feeling pain. I can feel the pressure of the wood lodged in my shoulder, but I can also feel the warmth in the blood surrounding me. The noise is fading in and out, and flashes of light become blurry. He tried, he tried to save me, but was unsuccessful.

"We have to save her," Keelan cries.

The nerves in my body numb completely. I hear my heart slowly beat in my chest, slowly fading into nothing. This is how I'm going to die.

CHAPTER EIGHTEEN

KEELAN

Her limp body lay on the ground in a pool of her own blood. The bleeding doesn't cease. Her breathing is dangerously shallow, and her chest barely moves at all. Her eyes flutter, trying to keep herself awake. She can't give in to weakness.

"Juliet, wake up," I shake her. "You can't die."

I form my hands around the piece of wood. Michael rests his hand upon mine. We exchange looks, mine of despair, and his acceptance. He has given up. So easily he has given up.

"This can't be the end. Can't you do something? She is barely alive."

Michael rests his hand on Juliet.

"I cannot bring someone back to life. Once someone is dead, their soul goes to its place forever."

I don't know where Juliet would even go. She is of witch an angel, two things that don't mix together. Her mother sold her soul to Samael. Even Juliet summoned Samael back in Stull. So who's to say where her soul will end up?

"Juliet, please don't leave me. I love you."

I sob into Juliet. Fighting no longer interests me. I want a demon to strike me right now, rip open my chest and feed from me, devouring me into its belly. I want to die with the woman I love. Her broken and bloodied body is too much for me to bear. I am giving up. We die together.

"Juliet?"

I wipe my tears and peer behind Michael. Arthur, Bristol and Allister stand over us, terror-stricken. Arthur is completely healed from his sickness. He stands straight up, with more power and sturdiness than before. The blow to Lilith must have weakened her power over the immortals, but only for a short time.

"Is she?" Bristol hesitates.

I nod.

"You are her father, save her," Bristol shouts.

Michael shakes his head, "It is no longer in my power."

We stare at Juliet's dead body. So still, but so peaceful.

"However," Michael adds. "You are immortal. You have the power to change her in a moment's time."

"What are you saying?"

"Make her immortal. It may be the only way."

"She doesn't want that kind of life."

I doubt it could be done. Why would an angel tell me this? Aren't they against everything like me? I know Michael also wants to save Juliet, but the power is not with him, it is with me. I have to try. I'll do anything to give Juliet a fighting chance.

Samael and Lilth are preoccupied with the angels above us. Flashes of light race pass us, booming sounds shake the entire convent. They pay no attention to us below. For all they know, they could think Juliet is dead.

I pull the wood from her back and more blood pours out of her. I haul her into my arms, her limp body folds over my knees. I can feel the faint heartbeat in her chest. I hope to God this works.

I sink my teeth into her neck, only to release the venom inside of me. I can't give in to the euphoric high, for I fear I may lose control and kill her. Just when I think I have given her enough venom. I gently lay her back on the ground, straightening her body the way it was.

"Come on, Juliet." I press my palms against her chest. "Don't leave me."

Michael and the others stand around her, hoping to hear a gasp of breath or a beat of a heart. We all waited anxiously.

"It didn't work."

I wasn't fast enough to save her. If only I had transformed her sooner. She would still be here, fighting alongside the angels. I hate myself for ever believing this would work.

Her fingers twitch, and her body lifts from the ground like a feather. She's now levitating in the air in front of me. I'm too shocked to say anything or touch her. Her body levitates higher above us. The flying debris doesn't touch her, something like an invisible force field protects her.

Her wound heals itself, and the blood retreats into her body, and just like that, her body is healed. Like nothing had ever happened. Wings emerge from her back. They are not white like angels are depicted, but crimson like. She is becoming the part of her that was hidden for so long, an immortal angel.

As she stands before me, her eyes open. Her own consciousness is not there. Something else takes over her body. She is completely unaware of her actions, or maybe she is, she's just unable to do anything about it.

"Juliet?"

She opens her eyes. She has changed, and none like I have ever witnessed. She is a celestial being that can never die. Her blue eyes aren't blue anymore. Her right eye is black as night, and her left eye is bluer than ice. She almost doesn't look like herself anymore.

"She has merged with the angels and the immortal," Michael says. "She is an immortal Seraphim."

She is too beautiful to look away from. We lock eyes, but the feeling I once had changed. She looks peacefully destructive.The terror rises in all of us.

Juliet pushes past me and the others, her strength greater than mine. Her skin is cold like mine is. I listen carefully, her heart beats no more. Her chest is only a void now. Just like mine.

Juliet gracefully floats in the air towards Samael and Lilith. The demons attempt to tackle her, but they burst into flames if they get near her. They wail in her presence as they, too, are filled with fear.

Samael stops in his tracks, bewildered by Juliet's transformation. He falls to the ground and is completely vulnerable.

"Ruler of Darkness and the wicked, I banish you to a thousand years in the lake of fire. I call upon the name of Jesus Christ, to banish you back to hell."

Samael shudders in horror. His face turns to a bright red and singed with fire. His skin melts off his face. A pit of fire opens beneath the earth. The stone cracks under our feet, and it travels to Samael. He tries to crawl away, but the fire grabs him by the ankle and pulls him into the abyss.

Juliet looks to Lilith,

"You can't hurt me. I made you." Lilith cries as she stands up from the ashes.

"Shut it, you whore." Juliet reaches for Lilith's throat and lifts her with ease. Lilith struggles under the strength of Juliet. Her legs kick and squirm, trying to release herself from Juliet. Her claws rip open Juliet's skin, but it heals itself in a moment's time.

Juliet lifts Lilith over the fiery hole, and her body ignites in flames. Her piercing cry vibrates off the walls and shatters the remaining glass that is still intact. The demon who created us is now under the control of the immortal angel.

"O' Demon Lilith of the night. I banish you to hell for a thousand years, and a thousand years more, and forever. No more will you hurt the ones you created in the name of Satan."

Lilith's body drops into the fiery abyss, and the flames transform to blue. The ground begins to seal itself back to its original state. Everything becomes quiet. The sanctuary is still, and the ground rattles no more. A sense of peace washes over me, like I had been born again, and everything is new.

The angels blow their trumpets in victory and sore through the air with beams of light following them. Their swords roar with triumph.

I'm overwhelmed with emotion. My chest is filled with a sensation I have never felt before. The phantom beats in my chest are consistent. I hadn't felt the beat of a heart for so long I had almost forgotten what it was like to be alive.

JULIET

I fall to my knees as I break out of my trance. The bruises on my body have vanished, and the wooden debris has been removed from my back, and the hole has healed like it had never been there before. I reach for my face, tracing along the skin that was once burned. The scar isn't there anymore. The pentagram leaves no trace on my arm. There is no more pain.

"I did it," I breathe. "I banished them. They are no longer a threat to this world."

Keelan runs to me with open arms. Blood and ash cover his face. When we embrace, I notice I no longer feel the coldness of his skin. It's as if he was never a vampire. I let go of him, and I feel my own skin. The warmth has vanished. We both are at the same temperature.

I notice the red wings attached to my back. Veins line the seam where my skin and wings intertwine. They are incredibly heavy and uncomfortable. A warm sensation sits on the crown of my head. I reach for it, but nothing is there.

I'm an angel. I have transformed into a celestial being, just like my father. I never thought it would be possible; to be of dark and light. I know the part of me that was hidden for so long is the part I want to be. My life should be guided by the goodness I feel in my heart, and not by the evil my mother forced upon me.

How can I be here? I died, or I almost died. There's no way I could have survived from that much blood loss. My memory is unclear, and all I can see is blurry visions of the sanctuary chandeliers that hang above me. I remember Keelan's face covered in blood. Michael embraces me in his wings.

"How am I alive?" I pant.

He rubs his hands up and down my shoulders. He turns his face to the broken ground. I shake him from me. I listen to my surroundings. A soft hum surrounds us, but one thing I don't hear or feel is the beating of my heart. I bring my fingertips to my neck and try to feel a pulse. My chest fills with a void similar to Keelan's. My heart has stopped beating.

Keelan looks to the others, who stand behind him. The angels hover above us.

"Am I a vampire," I mutter.

"I saved you."

"Keelan. Am I one of you?"

He won't look me straight in the eye, almost like he is ashamed of something. *No, don't say it.*

"Yes."

My body over runs with emotions I can't control. Everything in me wants to rip his throat out. He knows this isn't a life that I want. I'd rather be dead than live as an immortal, feeding off people just to survive. Even though I love him, I still hate what he is.

"Why didn't you just let me die?" I cry.

Keelan steps away from me, hiding his face.

"I can't live without you, Juliet," He sobs. "But you saved us all."

He is so selfish.

Keelan points to our friends. Arthur, Allister and Bristol huddle together, and Michael stands inches away from them, unsure of what to do. The look on all of their faces tell me everything I needed to know before I continue.

Looking around the sanctuary, it's completely destroyed. The pews have been ripped from the bolts and the chandeliers are shattered all over the floor. Stained glass windows are broken, and it leaves only a hole in the wall now. A single crack runs between my feet and I follow it all the way to a figure of an enormous cross. The golden cross is still standing.

Michael runs to me, and the others follow. They surround me with loving hearts and emotions I can feel, too.

"I knew one day you would become an angel." Michael hugs me, whilst avoiding my new Seraphim wings.

"Why did this happen?" I cry into his chest.

"Your heart is pure, daughter. He knows where your heart is. He sees the evil that Esther gave you. "

"But how is this possible? I can't also be a vampire." I reach for my mouth to feel the fangs.

"I honestly cannot say. This goes against everything holy. God will be testing you. Be careful of your actions. He gave you these wings, don't give Him any reason to take them back."

A hunger pulses inside of me. My mouth becomes dry, and I long for some relief. Licking my lips only makes the hunger worse. I know what I need, but don't want to admit it. I've been repulsed by vampires for a long time, and now I am one. How can I live a life worth living if I couldn't even give myself the food I needed to survive?

"She needs to feed," Allister says.

Allister steps forward and reaches inside his jacket. He pulls out a small bag of blood.

"Boy, where did you get that?" Arthur asks.

"I always bring extra, to keep up my strength."

Arthur rolls his eyes, and Bristol's mouth drops.

Allister hands the bag to me. The blood is cold, not warm like I was hoping, but it will do. The blood splashes around the bag, free flowing, it almost makes me nauseous.

"You have to drink Juliet, or you will die. You can never be in the sunlight again if you don't drink." Keelan says.

I hold the bag of blood in my hands. If I don't drink it, then I'd die for sure. If I do drink it, then I'd be giving into the blood lust. I don't want to become a bloodthirsty monster. I don't want to be on the same level as evil as Esther.

I wonder if I'll ever see my father again. I will never die, so my soul will never have a resting place. And if I do unfortunately find a stake through my heart, I really don't expect to see the pearly white gates of heaven. I still believe my soul belongs to Samael, and I can't give him the satisfaction.

"Will I ever see you again?" I look up at Michael. Tears well up in the corner of his eyes.

"You will never die, but if you are to be stricken with a stake at any moment of your life, I do not know where you will go. You are part vampire now. It is hard to say what will happen."

"Whatever happens. I want you to know that I am beyond grateful for finally getting to meet you," I smile.

I lift the bag to my lips and let the blood trickle down my throat. It takes a moment to choke down, but after a few sips it tastes so refreshing. I crave more.

"I understand, daughter. It is my time to go now. The Lord calls for me."

"I hear him, the faint voice in the back of my head." I reply.

Michael smiles, because he knows I can hear the Lord, too. He reaches for my hand and kisses it before the beam of light sheds over him. His body disappears into small light particles almost like glitter, and he vanishes before my eyes. The rest of the angels return to their homes, along with Michael.

I already miss him, but I can't let it overcome me. I have to stay strong for him. I have finally met him, and I love him and that is all that matters. He will always look after me in spirit, even if he wasn't here in his physical body. I feel his presence.

A sense of relief and happiness washes over me. The convent is no longer evil. It's as if it had been consecrated all over again. Despite what I have done today, I still can't help but think something was left here on earth that shouldn't be.

Chapter Nineteen

The snow has begun to melt, but the chilly air still persists without fail. I carry a jar of dried flowers, roses, lavender and hydrangeas. I believed they'd keep better than real flowers in this weather, and much more sentimental than fake flowers. I open the jar to have one last whiff of the flowers before tightening the jar before laying it next to the grave.

"We gather here today to mourn our beloved friend, Victoria Mason."

Edith squeezes my hand and tries to choke back the tears. She is hurt more than anyone here, even Arthur. Edith has lost a sister, and I have lost an aunt.

"She was a very talented witch. She was clever and intelligent beyond comparison." Arthur trembles. "But most of all she is loved."

Victoria didn't have to sacrifice herself, but I;m not sure if we would still be alive if she hadn't. I vividly remember her face moments before she ran to sacrifice her life. It replays in my head like a movie stuck in a never ending loop. Her screams are nothing more than a scratching vinyl disc.

We have no physical body to mourn, we never found her body, only traces of her blood and strands of her hair. We only have her books, electronic equipment, and other trinkets she's collected over the years. Everyone decides to keep her belongings in a box, hidden away for safety. Arthur wants me to take her books, but I only see them as a danger now. I had almost died too many times under the hands of dark magic.

"Edith, would you like to say a few words?" Arthur asks.

Edith wipes away her tears and stands over Victoria's belongings. The candles' flames float in the air, like a glitch in the matrix; they don't move, but completely still.

"Sister, I wish I had more time with you. We fell apart, and I deeply regret not trying harder. I hope you forgive me in this lifetime and the next."

Edith's voice shakes, and I grab her hand to comfort her. Tears spill over the books. Edith grabs Arthur's hand, her act of empathy stuns him.

"I'm sure you are a good man. I am so sorry for the hatred my parents gave you. I can see the love in your eyes."

Arthur and Edith share emotions. I never thought I'd see the day when my aunt held hands with an immortal, let alone be in the same room as one. We all come together for one person we all love. I wouldn't have it any other way.

Arthur gathers Victoria's things and takes them to the car. He refuses to tell us where he's taking them. I catch him sneaking a mini journal into his coat pocket. I don't want to say anything. He probably took it for a good reason. We all want a piece of her to stay with us.

I return home with Edith. I needed to be away from everything supernatural. My body feels as if I have just fallen from an airplane miles high in the sky. My joints hurt and my head is still pounding. All I wanted was hot water cleansing me of all the trauma I have been through. I want to wash away all the blood and memories.

We arrive at Edith's new place. Much smaller than the house we lived in before. The house has the same vanilla scent to it as the old one did. It's so comforting. The temperature is just right, not too hot or too cold. The walls are painted white, and greenery lines the windows in almost every room. The window lets in a light that reminds me of my father. I had never felt more at home.

Edith shows me a new room. In it, a bed with a golden frame is perfectly made, with pillows stacked on top. The walls are painted a dark green. On the windows, there are blackout curtains, to block out all the sunlight. I lost all of my things in the fire, so I didn't have much, but this is a start.

"It isn't much. But I thought you could decorate it how you would like," Edith said.

"It's perfect. But how did you know I'd be back? Why didn't you just buy a one-bedroom house?"

She rests her hand on my shoulder.

"The angels talk, didn't I tell you?" She laughs.

She walks over to the closet and slides the door open. New clothes hang in the rod, the type of clothes I would rather wear more than the ones I'm wearing from Bristol. I was getting tired of the high end masterpieces. I want to thank Edith deeply for believing that I'd return, especially alive and not in a coffin. She spent money on me. Not knowing for sure if I would survive or not.

Below the shirts is a small table, decorated in an ornate cloth of red and gold colors. A wooden cross with vines carved into it sits on the corner of the table and next to it, a display stand. Edith pulls out an old photo in sepia color. It's a picture of Victoria. She looks no older than eighteen. She wears high-waisted bell bottoms and a striped long-sleeved shirt. Her hair is much different from how it is now, much longer.

"I found this in some old books." She hands me the picture. "I thought it would sit nicely on your altar."

Her kind gesture warms my heart, and a tingling sensation enters my chest. I know she has never approved of my witch heritage, and I never wanted to be like my mother, but now I can be like Victoria and my father. Edith's acceptance is all I ever wanted.

I place the picture neatly on the display stand and light the candle with the box of matches. The flame dances with excitement.

"I am beyond proud of you, Juliet." Edith wraps her arms around me. "Witch, angel or immortal, your heart is in the right place."

I admire the altar. The only thing missing is a photo of my father. That would put the whole thing together.

***

Keelan peaks over the tree trunk. He fidgets with his hands. It's just as nerve-wracking for him as it is for me.

"Are you sure you want to do this?" I stop Keelan behind a tree.

"I'm sure. We need to have a somewhat normal life. Why not do that with our friends?"

Keelan has decided to finally come forward to Regina and Brody. He knows exposing himself will be a shock to them. They both believed he had been dead for months now. Keelan wants to rekindle the friendship we once had. Although I agreed with him, there are fears I had about him making himself known. No one will take his fake death lightly.

"No one else can know," he mutters.

"They won't tell anyone." I pat his shoulder. "They know what I am. I trust them with this secret."

Keelan's body rolls around the trunk and walks forward with our hands clasped together. He breathes heavily, even though his lungs haven't worked for years now. The fibers in his body remember the feeling and anxiousness, and pure excitement.

In the field before us, Regina and Brody stand clueless. They turn to see us. Brody's arms fall to his sides. Regina wipes her face with tears. She runs to us with arms open, and her long blonde hair flowing through the wind.

After Samael had forced me to do this ritual. I found out that Regina was never there.I confronted her about it soon after. She had no recollection of the ritual. It's possible Samael wiped her mind, but that would be too nice of him. It's more reasonable to say she was just an illusion, to trick me into summoning Lilith. Although I'm glad she wasn't present. Her voice crying out still haunts me. It still could have been real.

"I knew it." she pulls Keelan and me to her. "I knew you were alive."

Her tears are full of raw emotion. She grabs Keelan and me tighter. Tears form in my eyes. I never thought we would be reunited. Weeks ago, I thought my life would have ended. Now that we've come forward, I'm ready to live our lives literally forever.

"Keelan. I knew I saw you the night at the club. You looked terrified."

Regina lets go of me and hugs Keelan full on. I see Brody in my peripheral vision. He doesn't take his eyes off Keelan. He's almost unsure of what to say. What do you say in this situation? He has lived life knowing Keelan was dead, and now he's there in the flesh.

"Brody."

"How are you alive?" Brody trembles. He is pale as a ghost.

Keelan stands face to face with Brody now. He doesn't take his eyes off him, and watches his every move. At any moment, Brody could run away in fear, but his entire body is stiff. Imagine knowing your best friend is dead and come to find he's been alive this whole time, and a vampire.

"It is so hard to explain to you, but you must know that no one can know about us."

Brody touches Keelan's shoulder. He shivers at the touch.

"You're alive. This is impossible," Brody insists.

"Juliet, told me everything by the way."

Brody releases the tension from his shoulders. His eyes swell with tears. I have never seen him cry with so much emotion. He had been keeping it bottled up for so long.

"I am beyond sorry for kissing Juliet."

Keelan's eyes widen. He squeezed his hands into a fist.

"You what?" Keelan shoots his eyes. "You failed to mention that tiny detail."

"It was my fault, Keelan. I was drunk. I pushed her too far," he turns to me. "However, I cannot ask for your forgiveness enough for all the rumors I spread. I know you didn't kill Keelan. I have always known it."

Our reunification is long overdue. It feels so great to finally be myself, and for Keelan to come forward. He knew life would never go back to normal, but our friendship is a start to a normal life. What is a life worth living without friends?

Brody and Regina didn't take it lightly that I was now an angel, not just an angel, but a Seraphim. They know I'm a witch, but they would have never guessed I had transformed into a celestial being. Regina almost didn't believe me when I told her I was an immortal. Brody would believe me if I told him I was also a troll.

It would take them both time to process the changes.

Regina and Brody leave the field together. We wanted a private meeting away from society. In fear someone may see the both of us, the town already thinks we're dead. We can't risk it with people knowing what we are. We trust Regina and Brody, but it's the others we don't trust. Humans lack the capacity to not be curious. I understand it was human nature, but our lives are so much different now.

"What is going to happen when we never age, and everyone we love dies?" I ask Keelan.

He sits in front of me, legs crossed. He picks at the grass.

"I've never stuck around long enough with someone to know what that was like. My family died before me, before I became a vampire. I mean, of course, people I knew passed away, but we moved so many times. I tried to close myself off to avoid the heartbreak. Then I met you, and I couldn't stay away."

His voice quivers.

"So I'll watch Edith die, and Regina and Brody too?"

"That is, if you want to stay here long enough to see them pass." He looks up to me. His perfect eyes gaze into my soul. "It's heartbreaking, to say the least. But it may be better to leave, knowing they love you, and you will become a memory to them. It takes time to grieve. Who knows how long that grieving will take?"

"Are you telling me I should leave the city?"

"No, it is your choice. But just know that people will start to suspect you. You can't be around all the time. You will never age, while people you have known for years deteriorate into nothing."

This is the side of immortality I never wanted to face. I know one day Edith will be gone and continue her life in heaven, but I never thought I would be the one to outlive her or any of my friends. The thought of continuing my life without them just seems like a miserable life. But Keelan did it, and he still does it to this day. Watching his own family die broke his heart. He outlived them. He still mourns for them. So how long will it actually take for me to grieve?

"It seems like a very lonely life."

"It is, but it wouldn't be if you had someone to spend the rest of your life with," Keelan says.

"I want you. Forever, Keelan." I pull his hands into my lap. "I went almost a year without you, and it was heartbreaking. Not a day went by that I didn't miss you. You're not just my best friend anymore. You are so much more than that now."

He reaches behind my neck and pulls me to his lips. I want this forever. I want him by my side forever. I want to travel to places I have never been before, with him by my side. I know I'm sure of it, because he never left me, even when I left him to sacrifice myself to Samael.

I know I'll eventually have to say my goodbyes to them all. It's going to be the most difficult thing I've ever done. There is no preparing for heartbreak like this. I can still keep in contact with them for years to come. But I will never be able to show my face in this town again.

"I know a place in Italy that you would love." Keelan smiles. *"I'd give the world for my Juliet."*

SEVERAL MONTHS LATER

We have been at this for hours now. I've lost track of time. I don't know if it's morning or night. My ears hurt from the constant screaming. My feet ache from standing and running around like a maniac. I don't know how much longer I can take this. I don't know how much longer Keelan can handle this.

Blood drips from his mouth. The whites of his eyes have turned black. I can't look him in the eye without feeling nauseous. Dried blood sits under his fingernails, all from attempting to claw his way through the chair.

"Keelan, fight back. Don't let him in. I know you can hear me," I shout.

He wiggles in the chair, chipping the wood off the legs. The veins in his arms become enlarged, almost bulging out of his skin. He laughs in a voice that isn't his. It catches me off guard. I look at Father Luca, who's holding the cross in front of his body.

"Demon, leave this body."

The demon in Keelan's body laughs in a low growl. Blood covers his teeth in a crimson mess. He licks his lips seductively.

"I never loved you, Juliet."

I try to tune out the words. "You aren't Keelan. Leave this body, you unholy being."

The demon laughs uncontrollably, and so loudly Father Luca stuffs Keelan's mouth with an old rag. Muffled noises still escape his mouth.

Two men standing by take hold of Keelan's arms and re-tie the straps that bind him. Keelan wiggles in his seat.

"Please, Juliet. I'm okay now. Let me go."

"Don't listen to him. He speaks in sin," Father Luca says.

Keelan rolls his neck, almost too far than should be possible.

"Who are you, demon?" I shout.

"Nice to see you again, Juliet."

www.ingramcontent.com/pod-product-compliance
Lightning Source LLC
Chambersburg PA
CBHW021135110726
47900CB00002B/369